CARMEN DOG

Other books by Carol Emshwiller

Joy in Our Cause
Verging on the Pertinent

CARMEN DOG

CAROL EMSHWILLER

Mercury House, Incorporated
San Francisco

Copyright © 1990 by Carol Emshwiller

Published in the United States by
Mercury House
San Francisco, California

Distributed to the trade by
Consortium Book Sales & Distribution, Inc.
St. Paul, Minnesota

Mercury House and colophon are registered trademarks
of Mercury House, Incorporated

Manufactured in the United States of America

Library of Congress Cataloging-in-Publication Data

Emshwiller, Carol.
  Carmen dog : a novel / Carol Emshwiller.
    p. cm.
  ISBN 0-916515-70-2 : $15.95
  ISBN 0-916515-77-X (pbk.) : $9.95
  I. Title.
PS3555.M54C3   1990
8123'.54 – dc20

89–27616
CIP

To Ed

Acknowledgments

Chapter opening quotes are from the following sources:

Chapter I	Newscaster, CBS, 1982
Chapter II	*Music Sketches* by H. Sherwood Vining
Chapter III	*The Garden of Epicurus* by Anatole France (Dodd, Mead, n.d.)
Chapter IV and XXI	*The transformation of Lucius otherwise known as The golden ass* by Lucius Apuleius, translated by Robert Graves (Farrar, Straus and Giroux, 1951)
Chapter V	*Justine* by the Marquis de Sade
Chapter VI	Richard Brinsley Sheridan
Chapter VII	A letter from Elizabeth Barrett to Robert Browning
Chapters VIII, XII, XIII, XVI, and XIX	*The Portable Nietzsche,* translated and edited by Walter Kaufmann (Viking, 1968)
Chapter IX	*The Greatest Adventure* by John Taine (E. P. Dutton, 1929)

Contents

CHAPTER I
Outlandish Changes

There is more matter in the universe
than we at first thought.

CBS newscaster

"The beast changes to a woman or the woman changes to a beast," the doctor says. "In her case it is certainly the latter since she has been, on the whole, quite passable as a human being up to the present moment. There may be hundreds of these creatures already among us. No way to tell for sure how many."

The husband feigns surprise. Actually he's seen more than he's telling, and right in his own home.

"But they are, it is clear, here among us now in many varied forms and already voicing strange opinions: some in love with water, rain, the tides; breathing heavily (as she does); while others quite the opposite, more like birds or foxes. Yesterday I saw one I thought quite like a giant sloth, upside down in the lower branches of a tree. Some are, you know, on the way up, others the reverse. As I said: woman to beast, beast to woman, and not much point to it all it seems to me. Marcus Aurelius wrote, and I quote: 'Is the ball itself bettered by its upward flight? Is it any worse as it comes down?' When did you first suspect your wife?"

" . . . her mouth grown wide, lips dark, her eyes suspicious. She smells — I don't know — like something from a marsh. Has become irritable. More so than usual. Whimpers. Drops things. Or, on the other hand, like a snapping turtle, sometimes won't let go. Drinks too much. . . ."

"Of course all this would be perfectly normal in a woman twice her age, but since she's only thirty-four, I think it's a good

1

idea to see a psychotherapist at once, both of you. You say she was a fairly good wife and mother, though somewhat irritating at times, and you want her back that way as soon as possible? You must realize, however, that she is at this very moment in a period of profound change, both physical and psychological. Be surprised at nothing. To my mind it is as if they all had eaten an apple from the tree of a different kind of knowledge and have seen with new eyes, not that they are naked, but have seen that they are clothed."

What the doctor doesn't mention is how many similar cases he's seen and just how far some of them have progressed. He doesn't realize that the husband wouldn't be a bit surprised, that the husband realizes from personal experience that some of the women are already talking in grunts (if at all), while others, who used to speak only in guttural mutterings, are now mouthing long, erudite words such as teleological, hymenopterology, omphalos, and quagmire.

Christine, for instance, red-headed, plump Christine, who had several times been taken for an orangutan, can now argue her way out of any zoo no matter what the educational level of the keepers. Mona, on the other hand, can almost fly (though it is unlikely that she ever really will). Her husband complains that she makes funny noises, but her children like her all the better for it. John is divorcing Lucille in order to marry Betty (quite bearish still, but evidently what John wants). Mabel has only recently been given a name at all.

This is not the case with Pooch, who has had a name from the start and who now finds herself taking over more and more of the housework and baby-sitting, yet continues to be faithful. Her mistress is deteriorating rapidly—mouth grown wide, eyes suspicious. Her master (the man who visited the doctor, as mentioned a moment ago) has tried all the experts he can afford and they are now, both of them, in psychotherapy, as the doctor recommended, but it looks as though the marriage can't last.

In other homes, similar dramas are playing themselves out in various ways. A guinea pig named Cucumber (because of her shape, and sometimes affectionately referred to as "Pickle"), although not very smart, is taking over several of the easier tasks in the house next door. Cucumber has spoken to Pooch on several occasions, but Pooch finds it hard to be with her because she feels that she, Pooch, needs to hold herself back. Sometimes she feels she'd like to grab hold of Cucumber by the back of the neck and give her a good shake. And for no reason. Phillip, the king snake down the block, has turned out to be female after all, as has Humphrey the iguana. Neither of them, it is clear, has much maternal instinct, though, and they were last seen heading south on Route 95 with not so much as a good-bye kiss to the little ones who had watched over them tenderly, albeit not very consistently.

On the other hand, Pooch is doing the best she can for her foster family. (The mistress has taken to drink and sleeps a good bit of the day, but bites out viciously if provoked. Not that she hasn't done something of the sort to some degree all her life, but before it had usually been a quick slap.) Pooch now does the shopping as well as the laundry, diapering, and much of the cooking, though she is hardly as old as the oldest child she's looking after. Pooch, who had always been smiling and playful, now has become serious and sad, watching over everything with her big, golden-brown, color-blind eyes.

The psychologist has counseled patience and forbearance on the part of the family toward the mistress, wife, and mother. Pooch, who has never been patient, realizes the importance of this and conducts herself with a quiet dignity far beyond her years—always her mouth half open, always a little breathless. It's not unattractive.

Lately she has been yearning to see the psychologist herself. After all, it is she who has taken on more of the burdens of the family than could ever have been expected. But a visit is out of the question: the therapy is already straining the family's finances to the limit, even though the therapist is giving them a discount and the first few months were paid for by insurance. But at last the day comes when the psychologist himself asks to see Pooch. He has, no doubt, come to realize that she is a key figure in the dynamics of this tormented nuclear family and that she is probably the most stable element in it.

He understands a lot of things about her just by looking. Right away he senses her suffering (how she sits, demure, her arms around herself, held in, or rather, held together). And right away he guesses that she has been dependent all her life. Guesses, also, that there was some sort of break with her mother at an early age (how her hands hover around her mouth, her bitten nails), and that her toilet training may have been inordinately severe, possibly involving corporal punishment (her guilty look and the fact that, at first, she cannot talk to him at all). Of course these are only conjectures.

He asks her for her dreams. She remembers only a short one of rabbits. He asks her about her hopes and fears. . . . And has she no ambitions, no hobbies, no interests beyond the immediate family? It seems not. He asks about her youthful indiscretions. She says, None, but what she doesn't tell him is her sudden guilty yet happy memory of having pulled woolen caps and mittens off the heads and hands of small children or grabbing the fringe of their scarves. At the end of the session he tells her to do something for herself every day, if only just one small thing: take half an hour off to do something she wants to do, eat a tidbit of a favorite food, buy a small, inexpensive gift for herself, or perhaps even something expensive. Play a game of frisbee. This is orders, he says, doctor's orders.

Psychologically he cannot be sure that he is giving her the proper advice. It is clear that Pooch has always wanted to be of service to mankind in any way that she possibly can. From the general look of her, he guesses that her retrieving instincts are strong and that she might be passionately interested in swimming. Perhaps she can have no other joys but these.

★ ★ ★

For the first few days after this session, Pooch does not dare follow his advice. Besides, she can't think of anything she wants or wants to do. But on the fourth day, on a whim, she buys herself a three-dollar bunch of daisies.

Had she a room of her own she would have put the daisies there, but she sleeps on the doormat. No one has thought to change this situation. No one has noticed her budding femininity . . . no one in the family, that is. And after all, the house *is* small. Hardly enough room for the parents and the three children. So there's nothing for it but to put the daisies in the kitchen, where she spends most of her time anyway. But later on her mistress comes in and eats the heads off all but one, leaving only an ugly bunch of stems. Pooch blames herself for this, for having been a little late in preparing supper. She props up the remaining flower in a small glass, but it's too damaged to stand straight. Pooch gives up and eats the last flower herself. She is the one, then, caught with leaves sticking out of her mouth and accused by her master of ruining the whole bouquet. He slaps her several times with a rolled-up newspaper and does not wonder where the flowers came from in the first place.

★   ★   ★

The psychologist sees Pooch for another session. This time he draws a picture for her of her id, ego, and superego, and explains to her that she should let the id have a little fun now and then. It's hard for Pooch to understand any of this, but she takes the diagram home and puts it in the only safe place she has, under the doormat. At night, when everyone is in bed, she takes it out and puzzles over the three circles that are supposed to represent herself, and the squiggles under them that are words. *Id,* then, is one of the first words she learns to read. After that, her reading progresses rapidly.

★   ★   ★

A few weeks later the mistress bites the baby. Not only bites it, but refuses to let go until Pooch puts a lit match to her neck. Now the baby's arm has a large, V-shaped wound. Pooch is terrified. First of all, she knows that she will be blamed and that this is a serious offense that calls for more than a few taps on the head with a newspaper — which Pooch has never resented, knowing full well that, in some sense, she deserved them even when she hadn't done anything wrong. (Of course she deserved no such thing, but low self-esteem has always been one of her main problems, as the psychotherapist well knows.) But now she is sure that a few slaps will not suffice. Also she has heard about neighboring creatures who were taken to the pound and never came back. Recently several of her rapidly changing friends have suffered just such a fate (whatever it is), having become too hard to handle at home in all sorts of ways. However one may enjoy the possession of an intelligent animal, too much intelligence, too many pertinent and impertinent questions, and too much independence are always hard to put up with in others, and especially in a creature one keeps partly for the enhancement of one's own self-image.

And then, of course, Pooch is worried about the baby. What will the mistress do next? Pooch knows that she must not let the baby out of her sight even for a minute. She has always had deep feelings for the baby, above all the other children. The psychologist would certainly say that it is because she was taken from her own mother at such an early age and that she needs to mother the baby to make up for her sense of loss. A fairly common reaction.

After seeing that the mistress, looking even darker and more bloated than ever, has fallen asleep in the bathtub, as is usual at this time of day, and that the baby, also as usual, is down for its nap, Pooch sits in her master's favorite chair to think things out. She has, from the beginning, been forbidden the use of this chair, but now she deliberately curls up in it. She longs to lay her head on her master's knee and to look up at him, letting all her yearning speak out to him from her eyes as she used to do. She wonders if all these new words she's learned are getting in the way. Life was so much happier before she knew so many of them. It was at just such times as those, her head on his knee, that the master used to talk and talk, stroking her and telling her that she alone understood him and accepted him just as he was. And she did, if not understand completely, at least accept completely, and still does, though it's been a long time since he has sat here with her on the floor beside him. Perhaps she knows too many words now for him to speak so frankly. Perhaps he suspects that, now that she knows the words, she may *not* understand and may judge him more severely. But perhaps she, too, has played a part in the fact that this no longer goes on, both of them, on some deep level, realizing the impropriety of the stroking of the head and the scratching behind the ears of a nubile young woman by the man who is, even if not a blood relative, to some degree in the role of her father.

And Pooch *is* growing into a fine young woman: slender fingers where her paws once were, cheeks covered with little more than a peachy down. She is, after all, pedigreed, which is more than one can say for her adopted family. She was born on a farm, but no ordinary farm — as a matter of fact, a very famous farm in Virginia. Her father was from England and of impeccable bloodlines and her mother's family had been registered for generations. Also the psychologist is right, she had been torn from her mother at quite an early age by her master and mistress. They had been on a vacation trip to Florida and had stopped off at the farm to pick up Pooch on their way home to Long Island; they could not have been expected to wait until she was of a proper age to leave her mother.

Pooch is aware by now that she has been living not far from a major urban center that is full of opportunities as well as dangers. She thought about this when the psychologist asked her what she wanted to do with her life, because immediately the idea popped into her head that she wanted some sort of career in music and that she lived not far from some of the best singing coaches in the world. She isn't sure if she has any musical talent, even though from an early age she took every opportunity she had to listen to good music and to sing along with it. Her master and mistress soon put a stop to that, however, commenting on her terrible voice, which made her feel very sad. But the yearning still remains, if anything all the stronger for being suppressed, though she had put it completely out of her mind until the psychologist asked her what sort of (happy) future she envisioned for herself.

What she saw for just an instant was herself as Carmen, all in red, the rose in her mouth, dancing the seguidilla, though Carmen is quite the opposite of Pooch's general personality, which is basically (and becomingly) modest. (She is also petite; what's left of her fur, mostly white with flecks of black; long silky ears, one golden; small feet; noble head. She has a slight stutter, though never when she sings. Sometimes the words won't come at all. It is at these times that her eyes speak most eloquently, as though just by staring and cocking her head she could make herself understood. Her feelings about sexuality and loyalty are decidedly old-fashioned. Once she marries, one can be sure that she will never stray.)

Now, however, it is clear that she must leave her beloved master and it is clear that there is nothing for it but that she take the baby with her.

What Pooch doesn't realize is that, at this very moment, there is nothing in the bathtub but a very large, very vicious, and very drunk snapping turtle and that when the husband comes back in the evening he will understand the whole situation at a glance and will consider his marriage vows to be henceforth invalid and also his financial obligation to his wife at an end. Their bickerings had degenerated to incomprehensible mouthings anyway, and their lovemaking, though they had kept on with it in spite of increasing difficulties, had become mutually dissatisfying. So it will be with a sense of relief that he will take the creature to the nearest aquarium. And rather proudly, too, to be able to contribute what may be perhaps one of the largest snapping turtles in the world, a gift from him to the community at large. Also he wonders about her dollar value, whether she might be some sort of tax write-off and, if so, how much?

Pooch had run away a few times before, but that was when she was much younger. She had always been found in the neighborhood, her master driving around block after block until he discovered her in some backyard not far from home. After disposing of his wife, he proceeds to search for Pooch in his usual way, little dreaming that she is already in New York. After an hour of fruitless circling, he finally realizes that this time she is not to be found in this manner. His feelings for her begin to change as he realizes that she would no longer, could not possibly any longer, be wandering about in someone's yard behind the lilacs.

He understands finally that it is a desirable young woman he is looking for, and the more he thinks about it the more desirable she becomes. What's more, she's his. He picked her out, bought her, trained her, taught her everything she knows (or so he thinks, anyway), disciplined her, took her — or used to take her — for walks. . . . And what a good hard worker she has turned out to be in the end! How sweet and uncomplaining! Just the sort of wife he always wanted. Never once an argument the whole of her life with him. He is thinking how all might be, at last, harmonious. Life could begin again with her beside him. Perhaps it could be a time of new and strange excesses he never dared even to think about, let alone perform when he was younger or with his wife (who always rather frightened him) for, after all, Pooch is another kind of creature entirely. Courage would hardly be needed with such as her. If, for instance, he wanted to tie her, spread-eagled, to the bed, she would not wonder at this behavior. He decides to call the police as well as missing persons and tell them that it is his wife who has run off with their child . . . his beautiful young wife.

★ ★ ★

Why is it, the doctor has been wondering (along with many other professional people), why is it that only the females of the various species are affected by all this changing? Why have no males, as far as has been ascertained, been changing too? Surely if extraterrestrial dust or some such substance had dropped from distant stars, the men could not have avoided it. Perhaps it isn't of stellar origin at all, but atomic radiation, or maybe it's simply industrial waste. But the doctor and other professionals would rather think about the stars, and do—or else about the moon, for haven't women always been influenced by it? Perhaps it has changed in some way since being stepped on, especially a giant step by a *man*. Specialists in women's problems have been called upon, ad hoc committees set up. The scholarly journals are full of conjectures, but no good answers or solutions have been forthcoming except that perhaps all the women should be inoculated with male hormones.

The doctor thinks it is a simple question of willpower . . . a case of mind over matter (males), or matter over mind (females), and this very lack of willpower, he believes, is a form of aggression. Females, then, the worm in the apple, as ever; or rather, the first bite into it. Always—even before all this happened—in a state of disequilibrium; exaggerating themselves and their plight, sighing, braying, little cries of *ai, ai, vey, vey, piu, piu, oh, ow, poo,* and so forth. What difference does it make, when all is said and done, he is thinking, that they take the shapes when they already have had the sounds down pat for so long? And what passionate undercurrents in all these voices! (He has often found them downright embarrassing . . . even his own mother, though not, thank God, his wife.) Passion has always been their undoing, while he himself has always been ruled by the intellect. More even than most men, so perhaps (he thinks) he is the one uniquely chosen to return the world to its former comfortable dependability.

A few simple experiments may suffice to prove his willpower theory. Then it would simply be a matter of finding the leaders—those who have instigated the others in this lack-of-willpower behavior—and retraining them with electric shocks or any sort of aversion therapy. Perhaps it can be done in his large, airy basement. Put up a few cages and section off a laboratory. Take in several homeless waifs and wives. Make sure they get a good breakfast. Surely many would be happy with little more than a roof over their heads. It's spring but it's still pretty cold outside at night. Certainly *they* won't cost much. It's the equipment that will be the major expense. He decides to apply for a grant at once.

He has read in Marcus Aurelius that "Matter in the universe is supple and compliant, and the Reason which controls it has no motive for ill-doing; for it is without malice, and does nothing with intent to injure, neither is anything harmed by it."

No, it is clear that it is not the fault of Matter at all, but of the female.

★   ★   ★

Lincoln Center on a Friday evening. The several audiences are strolling about in front of the fountain; have not, in fact, collected themselves into audiences at all, but still function basically as individuals or as couples. What a wonderful diversity exists among the women! What feathers, scales, and furs! What sounds! Laughs and shrieks that reach the highest C. Seeing them, one might wish also for banana women, apple women, pine-tree women, but one can't have everything and this suffices to all but the greediest seekers after life.

Pooch, before the splendor of Lincoln Center, watching the elegantly dressed women, is reminded of a Japanese poem:

Butterfly
Or falling leaf,
Which ought I to imitate
In my dancing?

and also a line from another poem: "Very little happiness would be enough."

She's had nothing to eat since morning, but, though it certainly would help to lift her spirits, food is not what she hungers for. As it happens, she receives exactly what she wants most of all. Or rather, the second best thing. Someone hands her a ticket he can't use. Not for the Metropolitan, but for the New York City Opera. Yet even this is beyond her wildest dreams, and by some strange quirk of fate, the opera is to be *Carmen*.

Pooch thanks God that the baby has had a hard day and is sound asleep. She tucks it under her arm much as one would carry a bunch of books and enters the theater panting slightly, short of breath from the excitement of it all. Her simple elegance belies her inappropriate clothes (ill-fitting jeans and torn, discarded sweater that once belonged to the oldest child of the family). She carries herself well and people notice her, though inside she is feeling small and spotted.

And so the opera begins, Pooch whimpering occasionally with a pleasure that cannot be contained. When Carmen sings: *"L'amour est un oiseau rebelle . . . that nobody can ever tame,"* Pooch is enraptured. Yes, it's so true, so true. That's just the way love is. She is thinking of the only males in her life (not counting the oldest child): her master and the psychotherapist, for whom she already has a full-blown transference.

But of course (as could have been predicted) it is Micaela's song that moves her most of all, even though her French is rudimentary. *"Je dis que rien ne m'épouvante"* and *"Seule en ce lieu sauvage . . . j'ai tort d'avoir peur; . . ."* bring tears to her eyes. Pooch might be said to be in somewhat the same fix that Micaela is in. Suddenly she can no longer contain herself and raises her voice in a mournful obbligato to that of the soprano on stage.

Everyone turns to look at the rear of the balcony, wondering where this strange sound is coming from. Pooch has the words all wrong, but they are emotionally correct and full of homesickness and fear. Her voice is obviously untrained but has a surprising power. Something spellbinding about it. Something wild. It has what Roland Barthes calls "grain": "(One hears only that)," he writes, "Beyond (or before) the meaning of the words . . . from deep down in the cavities, the muscles, the membranes, the cartilages . . ." The audience is, for just a moment, won over. The Micaela on stage stops singing, confused, and Pooch goes on by herself, her trembling audible. But this lasts only a minute, for the baby begins to cry. Of course Pooch is quickly hustled out amid catcalls, boos, and hisses. She hunches over in shame, the baby screaming.

Shortly afterward, and perhaps precipitated by the unforeseen commotion, the Carmen on stage begins to limp and whinny in a very strange manner. It is clear to all that she cannot be counted on to finish the opera. In truth, the impresario has been worried of late, wondering how to replace these highly trained but changing women. He has even, just for a moment, thought of castrating little boys to ensure a crop of sopranos for the future, but now he realizes that there is a better source he hadn't recognized. He rushes to the lobby to try to intercept Pooch before she can get away. Here, he is thinking, is something wild and new to work with, though will she be able to practice as hard as necessary, and with a baby no less? No doubt she is poor, but he will finance the training. He will put his foot down, though, on helping with day care. She will have to find resources of her own where that is concerned. Yes, there is power here that he has not heard before. But she's already gone by the time he gets to the door. "Find that woman," he yells to a ticket taker, but the young man is running off in the wrong direction.

It is unlikely that he would find her, anyway, since she is soon to be netted by the dog catcher; for, as she flies from the scene of her humiliation, she runs unthinking down the middle of the street, hardly aware of the honking. She is booked for chasing cars, though of course that was the farthest thing from her thoughts, but her protests are in vain. The pound is not exactly the place for a trial by a jury of one's peers, so she is summarily found guilty as charged. And as usual, she does have that guilty look. If only she had twenty-five dollars instead of two seventy-five in quarters (laundry money she hadn't even meant to take, but found in her pocket after she'd left—she would never take money on purpose, even when running away and even when it might have helped to feed the baby). Twenty-five dollars and she could buy her way out and no problem.

Worse yet, they know who she is and will notify her master first thing in the morning, for Pooch is still wearing her collar with the license on it. Being a law-abiding creature, she had not even considered taking it off.

CHAPTER II
In Which Pooch Becomes
a Vegetarian

Music . . . carries the soul captive
across the rough and stormy sea of life,
and stands beyond the vale of time to
welcome with angelic voice the wandering soul.

H. *Sherwood Vining*

The cages are quite cramped for those creatures who are becoming approximately the size and shape of humans, and of course
none of the cages is of a size to hold those tending toward bear or
elk. Pooch is squeezed into one on the second tier. At first they
don't know quite what to do with the baby. They are thinking
that perhaps it can be put up for adoption later if no one calls for
it within the week. Young things are always so cute they're hardly
ever hard to get rid of. One of the men there has it in his head
that Pooch, herself, may be valuable for quite different reasons.
He is thinking seriously of stealing her and taking her home
with him. He thinks that he might make quite a bit of money in
one of two possible ways: her breeding is obvious, and so is her
virginity. At any rate, for the time being, she goes into the cage
and they decide to put the baby in with her. That way it won't be
making a fuss. So the two are left with a bowl of water, a rather
dirty bowl in fact, and a dirty bowl of kibbles. Pooch is used to
such simple fare as this, having eaten little else all her life, though
now and then she's had a tidbit from the table, which frequently
she wished she hadn't had. It only whetted her appetite for
things she didn't dare allow herself. She is worrying about
the baby, though, and what about its vitamins! Now it refuses
all but a few mouthfuls of food. Yet it seems the little thing
is all screamed out and, thank goodness, soon falls asleep again
now that things have calmed down a little. Pooch is too despond-
ent to do more than curl up, hugging it to her budding breasts

14

(which are all coming in shapely, firm, and perky. The best kind).

Above her on the third tier is a brilliantly dressed creature, black, red, and yellow — or rather, what Pooch suspects are those colors, for red she cannot see at all (she has been warned about just such stripes as these) — and who, Pooch soon learns, calls herself Phillip and was picked up for hitchhiking on Route 95. Pooch got a good look at her while being helped up to her own cage. Phillip had looked back at Pooch with a rather scary, hypnotic stare and an ironic grin, tongue between her teeth. Of course, being underneath, Pooch can't see her now. She is trying to remember: "black to yellow, dangerous fellow" or is it "safe fellow" or "black to red, you're dead" or what? And which stripe *is* the red one? But considering that Phillip probably was at one time a pet Pooch thinks she's most likely perfectly safe. But what a gorgeous creature! What sinuous, serpentine grace!

As soon as they are locked in for the night, the bare bulbs blazing overhead, the whole place comes alive with the talk and attempts at talk on several levels of expertise. Phillip, it turns out, has been here longer than anyone else — almost a whole month. "There'th a reathon for that," she says, lisping seductively. Her tongue, of its own accord it seems, extends farther than is necessary to form the *esses*. "And you can get anything you want, ath I do. Better food, drink, thigaretteths. You name it, I get it. Not everybody can, but you can, Pooch. You have . . . well, nearly the figure for it and you carry yourself well, though you shouldn't look so shy. Men take you for how you present yourself, you know. You have to learn to use your body."

"Yes, but, but, but," Pooch answers, stuttering a bit more than usual because of her anxiety, "but whatever it is you do, it hasn't brought you any closer to escaping from this dreadful place."

"But will," Phillip says. "Will too, one of thethe dayth. Anyway, know what's going to happen tomorrow? You may have no choice but to do ath I do or elth."

"What?"

"All thothe who have been here over one week — not counting mythelf, that ith — all but me . . ."

At this moment a roar of rage from beneath them.

"You're a brute, Isabel," Phillip calls down, "and don't know it."

"Not so. I love. I always love, more and more."

Pooch wonders whether Isabel is referring to life in general that she loves, or to creatures in general, or to some particular creature. When Pooch had been brought in she had had only the slightest glimpse of sleek black hair, beady eyes, and sharp teeth from the cage below.

"At any rate," Phillip continues, "Love or not, Isabel, you will
· be taken off to that far room there along with theveral otherth. All female, by the way. If you'll notice, Pooch, the pound ith no longer for any but uth femaleth. And you'll be killed, Ithabel, and then dragged out through here in front of all of uth and out to a truck— I've theen it— then they will take you to be burned or uthed for fertilizer or maybe even made into dog food . . . kibbles, for all anyone knowth. All of you, unleth you do ath I do, or can do ath I do, though not all can."

And now groans, moans, and squawks from all over the room and a kind of yawn of rage from Isabel.

"It's political," someone shouts, "or cost-effective, and something must be done about it."

"Is this what they call a democracy?" Another voice.

"This never was *your* democracy anyway." Scornfully.

Pooch nearly throws up, thinking of the kibbles she has just gobbled so greedily. She decides she will not eat any sort of meat ever again and that she will especially not eat kibbles, whatever they may say is in them. She makes a silent vow to be a vegetarian from now on even if she has to starve to do it. Better that than even the remote possibility of eating one's friends and fellow sufferers. At the same time, she vows not to be lured into the kind of behavior Phillip is talking about, however much it may seem like something Carmen would do in a similar situation, and however much it may be of benefit to herself. She realizes that, though she would like to play at being Carmen and sing and dance the Carmen role, she herself is of quite the opposite nature. For instance, she is thinking that if she had had Don José in love with her, she, unlike Carmen, would have stuck with him in the first place and then the opera would have come out entirely differently and, Pooch realizes with a sudden little shiver of doubt, probably not even have begun at all . . . not got off the ground, or certainly have bogged down in the middle.

Yes, her kind of love is probably too true and steadfast for most people to put up with for very long, either in life or in art. Perhaps it scares them or makes them wonder about their own obligations, and of course it is quite out of fashion. Pooch knows that. Well, she thinks, I shall love my kind of love anyway, doggedly, for I must certainly do the best I can with my own nature and if my nature is to love too well or from afar or to be grateful for crumbs — as the psychotherapist put it, though at the time I thought he meant those scraps under the table, and I *was* grateful for them — well, so be it. But some day I will find a love that mirrors my own. Pooch resolves then and there to save herself until her true love comes along. For a few moments she falls into a deep and satisfying daydream common to female creatures of her age and experience, or rather inexperience, but soon these thoughts bring her back to thoughts of her beloved master. Certainly she will not be here long, only a few days, if that, because her master is to be notified in the morning. It's hard for Pooch to get the idea out of her head that when he comes, everything will be all right. She has to keep reminding herself that this is not the case at all, that it is she who ran off, and when he comes for her, here she will be with the bitten baby, as though having run off with the evidence. But if she apologizes profusely enough and promises to work much harder, to get up very early, eat less, and not take even one little moment for herself or even one little penny ever again for such frivolities as flowers (in spite of what the psychologist said), perhaps in this way she can make it up to him or do penance of some sort. "Anything," she will say to him, "I'll do absolutely anything: lick your feet, walk one step behind your left heel . . . just let me stay and serve you and let me see the baby now and then if only from a distance and, should the mistress bite me, all the better, then." She hopes that after she says all this and makes the promises, he'll see that she's worth keeping—a thought not uncommon to many creatures of her sex.

This is Pooch's first night away from home (though not away from the family, for she has often been left alone in the house for several days with nothing but a huge bowl of water—plus, of course, the toilet bowl if worse came to worst—and enough dry food for only one day in case she might overeat. No matter how much she protested that she had outgrown such excesses, they never did trust her not to make herself sick by eating the week's rations the moment they were out of sight. (Actually, she tried to make that one meal last as long as possible.) Those times were hard, but Pooch guarded the house very effectively while they were gone in spite of being half starved and feeling rather weak. And anyway, she could sing all day long if she wanted to, and did, and could play the music she preferred and listen to the Saturday afternoon opera.

Oh, the sweet smells of home, Pooch is thinking. Oh, the sweet, sweet, sweet, smells of home! The socks, the running shoes, the familiar crotches. And the states of mind, all so well known. Predictable emotions coming around in their predictable cycles. No rages not raged before under similar circumstances. But now, here, nothing but the unknown. Even the master. What will he do? Probably take the baby away and leave her here to be kibbled at the end of the week or to meet a fate like Phillip's, whether she consents to it or not (for she has seen that look in the eyes of the keepers; and the way she had been helped up to her cage was, to say the least, rather lewd). To distract herself from her depression, she tries to think up a Japanese poem of her own and finally, after some effort, comes to this:

Willow by the stream
leaves fall
two by two
two by two
Oh, will I ever love such a love?

She is glad she gave herself formal artistic limitations; otherwise, she is sure she would have put too much sentimentality into it for any real resonances, especially in her present state of mind.

Just then more yawn sounds from the cage below.

"Isabel's having one of her angry fith again," says Phillip; but to Pooch, who has always read between the emotional lines, so to speak, the sounds, while distinctly roars, seem more like cries for help.

"Shut up," says Phillip, "and let uth get some rest."

"Rest for what?" This from the top tier across the room. "Does one rest up to be in good shape to die in the morning?"

"Me. Was one of. Beautiful people," Isabel is saying.

"Look at yourthelf." Phillip.

"Had a waist. You'd not believe. Had a coat. Of wolverine."

"Now you have a permanent coat of wolverine. Nice and shiny, too."

"My heels, three inches high. Hairdresser said, never so fine a head of hair."

"Isabel, you committed dreadful crimeth and you know it. I wath here when you were booked." Phillip. "And I thaw your whole methy attempt to ethcape."

"If I hurt. Never meant to. Not before either. With all my wealth and beauty. Lots of times all I wanted was to die."

"Well, now you'll get your wish."

Incomprehensible animal sounds from below and, "Let her be," from across the room. "We all feel the way she does. All except you."

"I want to go on loving. I mean live. All the better now. I wanted to die. Not really, though. Now live on. Be. Be! I only just realize. One more change is all. One change! Once chance at it. I mean chance."

Pooch, as is frequently the case, is in the mood for a sacrifice. And surely her master will understand the gesture and appreciate her kindness . . . her humanity. Most of all that. Understand, at last, what she's capable of and love her all the more for it. And besides, would any creature who makes such a gesture as she is about to make ever have been able to bring herself to bite anyone, least of all a baby? Of course not!

Pooch takes off her collar and dangles it down from the bottom of her cage door so that it hangs in front of Isabel's cage. "Can you reach this?" She feels long, sharp fingernails scratch her hand and she can see, as they reach up, the half-worn-off red enamel.

"Hmm. Hmm." Then a triumphant, "Got it!"

"I'd suggest," Pooch says, "Th, th, th, that if he doesn't know what changes are which. I mean if he thinks you're me, stick with him for a while, but if he suspects something right away, then I suppose there's nothing for it but to tell the truth."

"Can do it," Isabel snaps back at her. "Let me out and I can do it. Always have. Will."

"Be . . . be . . . be kind to him. Promise me that. Remember, he's saving your life at least as much as I am."

"Will do."

"Promise."

"Did."

"You'll find him strict and a little bit domineering sometimes, and other times rather distanced — in fact off-putting until you get to know him. Stern, but *usually* fair. I must admit the mistress is difficult, but things are hard for her right now and the psychologist says be patient, so you must. You'll sleep on the doormat."

"Hah."

"Sometimes the bigger children pull ears, but they're young and. . . ."

"Oh, shut up. I'm tired. Big day. Tomorrow."

"Me too." From Phillip. She starts to say, "lots and lots," but changes it to, "a great deal to do," in order to avoid the *esses*.

But all the others are feeling sadder than ever for, though they have not heard all of the above conversation, which was carried on as quietly as the two could manage, whispering back and forth between their cages, the others know that Isabel is somehow saved. Now the room is full of talk and moans and howls, and Pooch is feeling herself more and more one with them. And who could sleep with such anxiety? What will the keepers make of her now? No collar? No home? Not belonging to anyone? As far as they can tell just a stray? She's hoping they will remember that they only just arrested her last night and not for anything serious. And that she's supposed to have a whole week to wait for possible adoption. And anyway, who would look after the baby for them? But what if they put the baby in with Isabel because of the collar! Pooch begins to whimper along with the others. What has she done! Perhaps her generous, self-sacrificing, humanitarian gesture was the worst thing of all. Yes, she is thinking, at times like these one really does need a physical release, just as Isabel was doing with her roaring out. The psychologist was right. It all must out, one way or another. Pooch wants to cry, scream and roar, or better yet, sing. Yes, sing. Perhaps she could help them all with a song or two. She had been listened to at the opera. Only for a moment, but actually taken seriously, the whole audience, held fast by her voice. *Her* voice alone! She could feel it. She would try that now. It might help them all. She begins rather tentatively with *"Elle a fui, la tourterelle!"* gaining confidence with every note, for the others become silent almost instantly. *"Ah! souvenir trop doux. Image trop cruelle. Hélas. . . . Mais elle est toujours fidèle. . . ."* Now their only sounds, little mews of appreciation. She goes on to Massenet's *"Pleurez, pleurez, mes yeux,"* singing out louder, filling the whole room, the whole pound in fact, with her song. Even the night man wakes up and listens.

"Then weep! O grief-worn eyes! And flow, sad shining tears. No ray of sun shall ever dry your flood so clear. If a hope yet remains, it is that death is near."

It's hard to say if it is her voice or her sensibility that holds them spellbound, the rise and fall from almost whisper, to wail, to deep-throated growls of sadness and pain. Whatever it is, it reminds them of home. Home, in its many and various forms — burrows, beaches, tops of trees, all kinds of homes — and they forget for a while the dirty bowls, the smell of urine, and their fate. Soon a few begin tentatively and then all join in (some are quite good; others can't sing even a little, but they join in nevertheless), a chorus of wails, with Pooch, as at the opera, in obbligato, her voice soaring out over all the others. But it's too much for the night man, finally, and one can't exactly blame him, for, though at first the sounds were strange and wondrous, in the end they degenerated into a cacaphony wherein one could distinguish, though barely, what seemed like clucks, hisses, moos, rusty gates, hastily applied brakes, rattles, clicks, almost as though of joy, and almost lost in all this, the faint cries of a baby.

The night man rushes in, slamming the door and using quite dreadful language. Some that Pooch — though now and then kicked and sworn at but never so as to raise any real bruises — some that Pooch had never heard before.

It takes a moment for the singing to die down completely, many, in their enthusiasm, not hearing the night man's shouts, but at last there's silence, except for the baby's cries, that is.

"Keep it this way," he says, "or I'll have you all dead right now."

"Tho what, now or later," says Phillip, who is not afraid of anyone, or at least pretends not to be.

"I'll show you, bitch," the watchman says and then goes to get his radio, which he had not been using anyway, being asleep — though he'd brought it to keep himself awake. Turns it to a rock-and-roll program. Leaves it fairly loud, but not loud enough to bother him two rooms beyond.

Now they will certainly be up all night, though there's not much left of it, and perhaps the baby would be keeping them up anyway. But the baby seems to like rock and roll and soon quiets down.

Pooch apologizes, but almost everyone is very kind. "It's not your fault," they say. "Our fault, too," and, "It was good while it lasted." It's hard to talk above the music though, and they're all tired now, so, covering their ears as best they can and in their own individual ways, with bits of their clothes, their little fingers, or by burrowing into the wood chips, they return to their separate miseries. Pooch and the baby lie with their heads in the far corner of the cage, Pooch's right hand covering the baby's top ear and her left arm curled under her so that her left hand covers her own ear. She lies, half dreaming, thinking of someday instigating sweeping reforms.

CHAPTER III
In the Nick of Time

> "Women are the greatest enemies of
> science, and the wise man ought to
> keep himself aloof from them."
> "In legitimate marriage also?"
> inquired my father.
> "Especially in legitimate marriage,"
> replied the philosopher.
>
> *Anatole France*

In the morning the day workers come in — an entirely different
set of men. The lights are turned out and the radio is taken home
by the night man. All the inmates are exhausted, of course. They
lie, drunk on lack of sleep, too tired to care what happens to
them, grateful only that the music has stopped at last.

★   ★   ★

The doctor has also been up all night. He's been trying to write
his grant application. He has decided to start off with a quote
from Marcus Aurelius:

"Think often of the bond that unites all things in the universe. All are, as it were, interwoven, and in consequence
linked in mutual affection; . . . That is the way in which
the universe has all things to its liking."

and to proceed with an analogy . . . a sort of warning:

Gentlemen, look up at the night sky and imagine the
whole Milky Way sliding sideways, out of kilter. An
equally dramatic loosening is occurring.

That should scare them (as if they weren't scared already, as they
should be).

Let us, for a moment, imagine the earth as a living being. What sort of being would it be? Consider the fickle forces of nature . . . the fluctuations wherein the very platforms of the continents are not to be counted on to stay in place from one era to another. Surely you must grant, then, that the earth is unquestionably female: the tides, the seasons, the moon, the changing courses of rivers, the erosion bit by bit by bit. . . And what is this earth up to now? What small hold it had on rationality in the past, it seems to have lost altogether. And *they*, being of the same sex as their planet (would that it were otherwise and that we had a truly rational planet less subject to moods and bad temper), *they* have surrendered to the changes. They have let themselves go.

In order to stress the confrontational aspect, he goes on thus:

Remember that the female has always been a formidable enemy both of society in general and of man in particular, as well as a formidable enemy of the rational. And now they are blundering onward, a menace not only to civilization and to life as we know it, but even to themselves. What, one wonders, are their ulterior motives? What are their objectives? And, most important, what is their plan of attack?

He already has the ending. It goes as follows:

I propose to build a sort of two-part cage connected to a computer, with electric shock plates on the floors of each side that can be used simultaneously or alternately. Also a dispensing machine from which one may receive either a reward or a chit of some sort to be saved up and used to purchase small necessities of which I plan to keep a stash. The experimental activities will take place in basement rooms that will be heavily shielded from contamination by the outside air and particularly by the moon.

It has occurred to the doctor that perhaps just a set of thumb-screws would be adequate for his purposes. They would be less expensive and take up much less room in the laboratory, but the cage would be a nice piece of equipment and would show the grant committee that their money had been well spent. Also he would have a nice control board with lots of dials and little buttons so that he could manage everything from his desk, quite like the pilot of a 747.

He rounds off the grant request with this last:

> I shudder to think what the world might degenerate into
> if studies of this sort are not carried out by qualified peo-
> ple such as myself—and quickly. In fact, the thought of
> what might become of us is so horrifying to me that a soft
> coo or the flutter of wings at my office window is enough
> to throw me into a deep depression.
> And what, gentlemen, tell me, what of motherhood!

The doctor attaches his curriculum vitae and sends the application out.

★   ★   ★

And now shouldn't he be taking a good look at his own wife? Been too busy to think about her for quite some time. House clean. Food good. Very good, in fact. Laundry always done. And over all these years, too. Really quite remarkable once one thinks about it. Perhaps ought to praise. Yet, perhaps better not to cheapen his praise on the everyday—on jobs that should, in fact, be taken for granted. Two reasons: one, she may no longer take her work for granted herself simply from the praise, which might make her think she was doing something unusual so that she would question it and perhaps stop. And two, she may come to expect praise—even daily praise—for doing her daily duties. That would be more than he could manage, especially in the midst of this most important research. (Actually there is a third reason, which is that the doctor would feel uncomfortable and rather shy doing something he hasn't done for such a long time.) But, he thinks, must keep an eye on her. Here is one of their kind close at hand, available for immediate study. Could even start today. But could get the others today, too. Where find them, those average, homeless females in their various states of change? How most cheaply round them up and with as little fuss as possible and without chasing after them in an undignified way in the streets with a net?

He has already spent several thousand dollars of his own with the expectation of being reimbursed by the grant committee. He has a cattle prod, a horse-nose-twister, several sets of handcuffs, an ear-splitting siren. If force is called for, then force there will be. We cannot afford long years of negotiations. He has actually seen three grown women in what were clearly their best hats, playing in a tree house. They were so sparkling and lively in their feathers, even in the midst of this chaos, that it seemed to him monstrous, unforgivable that they allowed their bestiality to take over so completely. Also, as part of his researches, he has been to Macy's, or rather, tried to go, but that store, with twice as many guards as usual, has become a haven for any strange creature with money to spend. He left quickly. Later tried Bloomingdale's. Found it somewhat better. At least they only let in those who were presentable and who had a modicum of dignity, though he noticed they had added the most outlandish clothes to a department on the third floor, and their lingerie department was so upsetting that he lost his scientific detachment and hurried through it with eyes averted. On the way out he found the jewelry department full of masks and feathers and necklaces of sharks' teeth or claws, plus a few shrunken heads. Clearly, haste in his research is called for.

His wife, at least, is subdued through all this, somber actually, as well she should be. No, he will not take her down to the basement as his first experiment. She can be of help to him in other ways, typing reports and tidying up the dayroom and the cages. She has already re-covered an old couch for the basement, contributed cushions, made curtains for the high (and soon to be closed off) windows, though all these frills, or most of them, must certainly be removed when the grant people come to inspect the place. It wouldn't look scientific. But it's obvious she's trying to help. He will let her.

★   ★   ★

Meanwhile, back at the pound, Pooch, under the name of Isabel, is wondering if she will live through the morning. Several of them have been lined up, including Pooch with the baby, but they are confused as to whether this is to be a lice check or death in the back room. Pooch asks Phillip if she will take the baby if this turns out to be "it" for the rest of them. Phillip says she hates babies, but that she will if nothing else can be found to do with it. Isabel says, "Love baby. Love it. OK. See to it. *Love* it," but Pooch feels that it would be better to leave the baby with Phillip, who hates babies, rather than with Isabel, who keeps talking about love and who, probably because of the difficult night, seems to have degenerated to little more than three-letter words. This is not really so surprising since every single one of the inmates is rather the worse off mentally at this point, even those who are on their way up the evolutionary scale.

The master has been notified and, it turns out, will not be coming to get his Pooch (Isabel) right away due to pressing business. Trusting her, he has told the keepers to put her on a Long Island Railroad train and to charge the ticket and the twenty-five-dollar fine to his Diner's Club card. He will, they tell Isabel, meet her at Wantagh and take her out to dinner and would she pick up a bottle of wine. Isabel, out of her cage now, is trying to convince the manager to let her go with the ticket money, but the more she talks, the more he wonders if she's capable of getting herself home alone.

"One of two way," she says, "so go now out and be in it. You say not go. I say fit to go. So do it in time and not for you to do it, too. But the money. Yes."

"Are you sure your name is Pooch?" the manager asks. He is beginning to suspect something wrong here.

"Is Pooch. You see me as I am. To be Pooch is to be me. To be me is to be Pooch."

"But I seem to remember you coming in here last week fighting."

"Not me." Isabel gets so angry she snaps at the manager. Mostly she misses. Just scratches the back of his hand a bit. She had managed to hold herself in check just in time, or rather, almost in time.

"To hell with you then," he says. "I don't care who you are." He charges an extra ten dollars to the master's Diner's Club card, hails a cab, and pushes her into it. "And I don't care what happens to you, just don't come back here or you'll be sorry."

"Am. Was." Isabel shouts back, and then, as the cab pulls out, "Ha, ha, not Pooch," but the manager, glad to be rid of her, gives her the finger.

Out of sight of the pound a moment later, Isabel takes off Pooch's collar and throws it out the window. Then she settles back, looking out with an elegant bored expression and picking bits of sawdust from her sleek black coat. "To the Pla . . . to the Pla . . . to the Pla . . . za," she tells the driver.

★   ★   ★

In the nick of time, and just after they had discovered that this lineup was *not* a lice check, they are informed that a kind gentleman has paid all their fines and, regardless of the nature of their crimes, this day's batch is to be released into his custody later on that very afternoon. Meanwhile, they are to return to their cages and wait quietly until the truck comes back from its daily roundup. Phillip begs to be let go with them, for they are all hoping this means freedom. "I'll give you a wonderful afternoon," she says to the keepers. It's her only bargaining power. "You will anyway," they tell her and immediately take her upstairs to the stockroom and visit her one by one, or as the case may be, two by two, or three by three, all afternoon until they are tired and careless, so it happens that just as the creatures to be rescued are lining up behind the truck, they see Phillip come snaking naked down the drainpipe. She joins the line when no one is looking and Pooch lends her the baby's blanket to hide not only her nakedness, but her brilliant black, yellow, and red self. Phillip is clearly exhausted and in pain, but is determined to escape with them. They hide her as best they can, and when the time comes they help her up into the truck.

Shortly after this, while they are riding along toward the kind gentleman's place, Pooch is delighted, as are they all, with the baby's first clearly distinguishable word: No.

CHAPTER IV
A New Home

> . . . if that ointment really does turn
> me into a bird, I'll have to steer clear of
> the town; owls are such unlucky birds
> that when one blunders into a house by
> mistake, everyone does his best to catch
> it and nail it with outspread wings to
> the doorpost.
>
> *Robert Graves*

It's quiet and it's clean and, though a basement, what with the sun slanting down through the west windows, the red and white flowered curtains, the freshly painted walls, it's actually quite cheerful and, unlike the pound, it smells good. On the wall in a prominent place there's an old-fashioned sampler with MOTHER in blue on a tan background. And on the couch an embroidered cushion with HOME IS BEST. There's a large, lumpy, gray lady, plump and plain, who seems to be managing everything and who brings them all fresh water in brand-new bowls. They take showers and then sit down to a simple supper of kibbles and canned cat food (tuna flavored), with orange juice and carrot cake, additions procured by the doctor's wife who is, of course, the lumpy gray lady. When she hears that Pooch is a vegetarian, she brings her a nice salad and some nuts and, for the baby, some milk and later on some clean dishcloths to use as diapers.

After that she takes all their names, "first names only, please," (though of course some only have first names anyway) for the name tags to be put over the doors of their cages. Pooch doesn't dare say she's Pooch in case she might get Isabel in trouble or jeopardize her chances with the master in some way, so she says she's Isabel. "My, my," the doctor's wife says, but mildly and without censure, "you have a very bad reputation. You were almost not allowed to come." Pooch hangs her head, too ashamed to answer. It's hard enough, she thinks, accepting the name Isabel, without being saddled with Isabel's violent deeds as well. Besides, she loves her name. So simple and unassuming. She likes it also for the musical *oo* sound of it. Sometimes when alone she used to sing her name over and over: *Pooooooooch, Pooooooooch.* Her only consolation now is that the name Isabel does have a real operatic flair to it. "Isabel the opera star" sounds better than "Pooch the opera star," even if less musical. But she has thought that, if and when she does become an opera star, she might Italianize her name and spell it *Pucci.*

"You may call me Rosemary," the doctor's wife tells them after learning all their names. Then she leaves them alone for the night, locking them into their cages — quite spacious ones compared to the pound, with cot and chamber pot in each, plus a little shelf and chair and bedside table. The doctor's wife locks the main door, and after that the laboratory door and finally the door to the basement.

Even though at first they were disappointed because they had thought they would be set free, this is, at least for the present, the next best thing. They decide to go to bed early, feeling relieved to be alive at all and in such a nice place as this, though many have their doubts. "It's still very much a prison," they say, "no matter how good the food or how clean and new the place is." Before they settle down, they have a short discussion about several things: Shouldn't the treatment at the pound be investigated? Might the kind gentleman help them with that? Why is the pound only for females? What animal does Rosemary remind them of (though no consensus on this)? Some say, won't it be rather dreary if we have to spend spring in a basement? But others remind them how brightly the late afternoon sun shone in even through those high little windows. What about the lack of exercise? And, most especially, when will they finally meet the kind gentleman into whose care they have been released and to whom they owe their lives? (Pooch is hoping he will be someone as worthy of loyalty as her former master, though perhaps because of what he's already done for them, saving them from certain death, she will be true to him anyway, no matter what sort of person he is.)

They are all too tired to talk long so, though the clock hardly says eight, they soon fall asleep. Little do they dream that the basement is bugged and that every word they said has been recorded, to be listened to by the doctor at his leisure. He is well aware that the creatures have, some of them, acute senses of smell and hearing, and he will not be so foolish as to place himself behind some sort of peephole.

In the morning the name tags are all ready. The doctor's wife had painted them the evening before, with flowers around the edges in red, white, tan, and green to match the decor of the dayroom. She is obviously quite an artist, though, as she tells them, she has had very little training. They all help tack the tags up on the cage doors and then stand back to admire their handiwork: Mary Ann, Basenji, Isabel (Pooch), then Phillip (they had maneuvered to get adjacent cages), Arista-cat (called Arista for short), Doris, Lucille, Dodo, Myna, Chatchka, Tootsie, etc. The doctor's wife has also made little flowered tags for them to pin on themselves. This they immediately do, and set about getting better acquainted with each other, the doctor's wife included, though she does seem rather the quiet observer. They have many questions to ask her, but she says she knows very little, that she really hasn't been paying much attention to the whole thing, but they suspect she knows more than she's letting on.

Pooch is quite taken with Basenji (perhaps because she's so quiet and so young), and with Lucille in spite of her degeneration and stupidity, and with Dodo. Arista seems rather aloof, as might be expected, and Mary Ann is quite grotesque and unappealing, but Pooch knows appearances can be deceiving and that beneath the most off-putting exterior there may beat a compassionate heart. She is willing to suspend judgment until she gets to know her better.

After becoming better acquainted with one another, they all take turns playing with the baby. Pooch is relieved to have some respite from caring for it, though of course she loves it dearly. This is the first real time she's had away from it almost since she began to take over the household chores. Luckily for the master and mistress, her capabilities began to manifest themselves at just about the time the baby was born. Pooch knows that, if it hadn't been for her, they would certainly have had to hire someone to come in to help look after it, since the mistress began to manifest the worst of her own changes at about that same time. Before the birth of the baby, Pooch had done only simple fetching and carrying, waited on the older children, also cleaned the bathrooms and washed the kitchen floor as soon as she was able to hold a mop. But then it became clear that she was able to do even quite complicated tasks and so the diapering, bottle washing, and nighttime feedings immediately became her special jobs. Now, here in the kind gentleman's basement, all the other inmates are virtually fighting over who gets to do what for the baby, even the washing of the diapers. To them it seems a privilege to take part in anything concerning the baby so that Pooch, though confined to the basement, actually feels freer than she ever has since being adopted by the master and mistress. Now she, along with the others, has plenty of time to examine the books in the small bookcase. Luckily, one is *Stories From the Great Operas,* and another, *One Hundred Best-Loved Poems.* Pooch immediately sets about memorizing the plots of operas and also poems that she had not known before.

They read the old newspapers, those who can. They tidy up, wash out their underwear, water the plants, take naps, and of course discuss their situation, though they take care now to do so only when the doctor's wife is out, which is really a good bit of the time. And so the first day passes.

Pooch, though grateful for the two books mentioned above and for the dictionary, is rather disappointed in the literature available. From the very first, or at least as far back as she can remember, she has always wanted to improve herself, yearning toward a life of the mind as well as a life surrounded by great music. Here the magazines are mostly *True Confessions* and the books mostly old romances. The others do enjoy them, though, and Pooch does not begrudge them these simple pleasures. She even helps them with the more difficult passages. Also, no one there likes the kind of music that Pooch likes best. (Yes, there is a small radio.) Sometimes the rock and roll nearly drives her out of her mind, though not when Phillip dances to it. Then it's worth the pain in her ears to watch that sinuous body twisting and turning to the harsh beat.

As for the newspapers, so far there has been nothing about their own predicament, that is, nothing about the changing females, and the papers are not *that* old. It is clear that, for the time being at least, there will be nothing. There seems to be a blindness to the whole business on the part of most of those of the opposite sex. Not a blindness exactly, but rather some desire to handle it as though it were not happening. Of course there was that first tacit enthusiasm for taking on new and exotic sexual partners from among the changing animals, for trying new positions impossible before, and for dropping off old partners into the woods or zoos or oceans, and saying nothing about it to anyone . . . going on as though all this were the most natural thing in the world. It was almost as though the men had at last found a world to their liking, in which they had even more control than before and in which relationships and responsibilities were less confining. After all, they merely involved dumb animals who were not worth consideration, politeness, time, effort, gifts. Of course some soon found out that this was not necessarily the case . . . many who were involved with wolves or geese or other species that mate for life got themselves into more trouble than they bargained for.

At any rate, most seem to be coping silently and, at times, desperately, trying to keep control of the situation in any way they can and, as can be seen from what is happening at the pound, many are involved in quite violent and deadly solutions. To be fair, however, one must admit that a small percentage of the men are trying to help out as best they can, both in bringing reason to chaos and also in bringing a little happiness or, at the very least, some small comforts, to everyone's lives — whether human or animal or half and half — inasmuch as such a thing may be possible.

A few days of rest and recuperation pass and finally the time comes when the doctor's wife tells them they are to prepare for visitors and that they will soon meet the doctor himself. They are all eager to have the chance, at last, to thank the kind gentleman for saving their lives and perhaps to talk to him about their futures. Each has a plan of her own for the continuation of her life: to one it is to be dropped off in the wilds of Canada near some beaver dam, to another it is to be left near some barn. Phillip isn't sure whether she wants a job in a disco or not. Pooch, of course, will mention opera, but most of all she will ask to be of service in any way she can, regardless of how menial the tasks.

★　★　★

From the doctor's log:

May 14: Windows closed off and quarters stripped of all frills except for the MOTHER sampler and the HOME IS BEST cushion. Most of Rosemary's contributions removed: newspapers, old magazines and books, plants, radio, lamp shades, curtains, cushions, etc. Also forks and spoons (had already vetoed knives). Had all name tags removed and subjects numbered instead: 101 to 119.

May 16: Entered dayroom for the first time with the grant committee. Am sure subjects did not know which one I was. They were all in their cages and wearing the new sterilized blue smocks I had purchased for them. Was told by examiners am sure to get grant money or most of it, and to go ahead and purchase computer and electrical equipment. Said it was already on order. They seemed pleased that no time is being wasted.

May 17: Interviewed each subject separately. Refused to answer any of their queries or to speak with them in any but the manner that I myself had outlined. Thought it best to remain entirely scientific. Asked each of them exactly the same questions and made sure to ask them in exactly the same manner. Then took pictures of them naked against a grid, front,

side, and back views in order to chart their changes.
Some could not stand up quite straight; but whether
to write down, "as yet" or "any more" am not sure,
but will soon find out. A good deal of nervous gig-
gling went on during this, though a few seemed to
find it painful and tried to hide behind their hands
or hair or feathers. Many looked as ridiculous as
Joshua trees, stiff in their embarrassment, but one or
two flaunted themselves before me.

When dealing with number 107, made sure to
have cattle prod handy and that she was handcuffed
before being brought in. Rosemary reported that she
had no trouble doing this. 107 seemed anxious to
please, even asked to be of help on the project in any
way she could. She's up to something, of course.
Probably can't wait to get her paws on these notes. I
assured her that she *was* going to be of help and simply went on asking the planned questions in the
prescribed way. She responded conscientiously
enough, though I know her gentleness is an act. She
could fool many people, but she doesn't fool me.
What's she trying to prove, and why? Am sure she
knows more than the others.

★　★　★

List of trick questions for the subjects at hand: (The doctor
will explain to the grant committee that the questions are pur-
posefully oblique and that this accounts for their rather cryptic
and inadvertently poetic qualities, and that this can't be helped.)

Would you rather be a falling leaf or the branch from
which it comes?
If the scenery were drab, would you dress to match it?
If you like men (or even if you don't), do you want to
be like them or do you want to be different from them? If
different, just *how* different?

If you saw a sparkling lake and, behind it, a snow-capped mountain, what would you do to try to become one with that view? Would it involve a hat?

If the lake, though very beautiful, were polluted, would you be inclined to change the lake or yourself to fit the lake?

If you laughed at a hat in a store window, would you then go in and buy it? If so, at what point would a hat become too laughable to buy?

What does the word *mother* mean to you? Is it funny?

Are *you* laughable? If so, explain.

The importance of these questions will be clear to anyone at all familiar with the situation.

The doctor resolves that, while remaining scientific in the strictest sense, he will strike out boldly with bold theories and with bold experiments, though he will be careful not to let his imagination take over in any way. We know now, he is thinking, the perils of *that* direction.

May 20:   Computer, electrical equipment, and testing cage arrived and were set up by experts. Tested the levels of shock and the general efficiency of the set-up with subject number 106. Loaded the dispenser with cupcakes and fruit juices. Wanted something cheaper, but wife is insisting on good nutrition and I believe she should be catered to as much as possible, at least for the present. [The doctor blanks out this last when he remembers that his wife will be typing these notes.] All seems to be in order. Was quite an ordeal. Certainly a full day's work. Was at it with 106 for almost seven hours, not counting the hour or two I spent before bringing her in. She kept inordinately quiet through it all. Am wondering why! But have resolved, anyway, to concentrate on subject number 107 instead, the one called Isabel.

> She knows something, I'm sure of it. Her behavior
> so belies her reputation.

Now the doctor stops writing and leans back to look out the window. He is thinking of number 108 — that beauty 108. A strange kind of beauty she is, too. He has discovered that she was not even on the list of those to come here and he wonders why Rosemary didn't mention this. Thinks maybe he should reprimand her, just to let her know he noticed. Though, on the other hand, it is rather nice to have 108 and her sinuous, suggestive behavior, even though her reasons for it are clear and she'll not be getting any special favors out of him.

★   ★   ★

It is the doctor himself who returns Basenji (106) to the dayroom and dumps her on the old couch (which is now covered with the same sterilized blue nylon as their smocks). He would have hired an assistant for such menial jobs as this, but he doesn't want any of his findings to leak out to anybody even remotely connected to the opposite sex, so he's doing all the work alone except for the help of his wife, whom he's sure will remain loyal if only out of her dependency on him. She seldom goes out except for groceries and has few friends, her best one now, luckily, dead. Also probably a good thing, in some ways, that her hips hurt her when she walks and that her hands are quite out of shape with arthritis. More so than ever, and recently he's noticed she's been looking quite thick in the neck. He'll get her some calcium and some cod liver oil capsules for the osteoporosis. Perhaps he should see to it that she drinks more milk. No doubt she will appreciate that small attention. Help to keep her loyal. But if she wanted to get even for some inadvertent slights on his part, she certainly could do great damage.

★   ★   ★

They all crowd around Basenji when the doctor leaves. She is utterly silent now, and will not or cannot answer any of their questions. When their names were changed to numbers and all the frills removed, that was a bitter realization to them all, and now Basenji's condition makes them realize that, grateful as they are to be alive, they have much to be concerned about still— perhaps even including their lives. And yet many of them were quite taken with the doctor and still are, even after this. They talk about him constantly: How tall! How thin! What secrets do the dark eyes hold? (One must remember that he is, after all, the only male around. Some even find his cruelty an attractive mystery and think perhaps they can change him through their love or their good example.)

Basenji seems to have quite given up. "Sing for her, Pooch," they say. (Suddenly they are calling her Pooch again. They have tried to remember to call her Isabel, but that name is so equated in their minds with someone nasty and quite the opposite of Pooch that they have found it hard to stick to it. And anyway, they do not have a strong feeling that Pooch needs to be Isabel.) And Pooch does sing. Just soft, simple lullabies, and the three or four best singers join in in harmony. (They had been practicing quite a bit just for the fun of it.) But it is hard to tell if Basenji even hears them or not.

That night, as they are being locked up, Pooch requests that Basenji be allowed to share her cage and Rosemary agrees. All night long Pooch holds, by turns and at the same time, both the baby and the trembling, unresponsive Basenji, who is also hardly more than a child. Pooch feels herself to be older sister to them both.

May 21: Questioned number 107 for five hours, both the subtle questions and direct questions about leaders, also word associations, but it took her no longer to respond to *knife, motherhood, gun, leader, plot, widower* than it did to *kitchen, glove, fairy tale.* She did hesitate on *flower* and *doormat.* I wonder why. Must check into. But not one decent reply to anything. Had no opportunity to use the rewards in the dispenser. After the first hours, violent, diffuse struggling, all four limbs and head with micturation (must confess had forgotten to allow her to go to the bathroom either before or during) and, as with the first subject, number 107 became more and more silent as the session went on so that, by the end, she appeared to have lost her voice altogether. Am all the more convinced that this subject is on the way up and is capable of both violence and leadership, in spite of her mild demeanor. Why else this stoicism?

Was exhausted after session and carried on the late afternoon researches outside where observed one female in grocery store gobbling up produce as fast as she could and then crawling out on all fours so as not to be seen at the checkout counter. Are there no depths to which these creatures will not stoop! Am reminded of Marcus Aurelius, who said, "How comes it that souls of no proficiency or learning are able to confound the adept and the sage?"

And now, leaning back and looking out the window, he is wondering what would be the best scheme that involves using that baby; what would be most profitable to his researches?

CHAPTER V
Daunted

May your crimes make you as happy as
your cruelties have made me suffer.
Marquis de Sade

Pooch and Basenji curl up again together in the same cage, and Phillip, though she has always said she hates children and has never willingly held the baby if anyone else was available to do so, has now taken it in with her for the night. Many of the others wanted to, but Phillip insisted and finally won out as Pooch's oldest and dearest friend (even though oldest only by the proximity of her cage both here and at the pound). Actually, for all Phillip's talk of hating the baby and for all her ignoring it, the baby has always been quite taken with her, sometimes clinging to her legs in its efforts to stand up and, since Phillip loves to sit on the floor, the baby is always squinching itself over to her (it can't as yet really crawl) and curling up in her lap. Phillip never pushes it away, though she also never acknowledges its presence. Perhaps it is her bright colors and smooth, dry skin that lure the baby, but also perhaps the baby, on some level, understands Phillip better even than she understands herself. Now, however, Phillip hugs the baby to her and pats at it distractedly, making soft, sibilant nonsense sounds, hardly aware she is doing so.

Pooch now clings to Basenji as much for herself as for the younger creature. Neither of them makes a sound. It is the others who are restless and sighing. Arista stares beyond her bars with blinking half-closed eyes, flexing her fingers. Dodo looks fierce and yet, now and then, utters a squeaky "Oh." Doris and Myna flutter aimlessly about their cages, feathers flying out beyond the bars. Myna's are drab, but Doris's are a brilliant green.

41

Mary Ann laughs a strange, nervous laugh and clumps about her four-by-eight cage on partially webbed feet. Whether she is tending toward duck or swan it's too early to tell. Now and again someone lets out a squawk or a whoop of some sort. Phillip leans, weaving her head back and forth over the baby. She has always looked rather dangerous and now she looks more so than ever. There are whisperings of plans for escape. None feasible. They wonder about whether Rosemary can be trusted or not or whether they have any choice but to trust her and does she or doesn't she seem changed lately, and, if changing, isn't she more likely to be on their side? Most are wishing that they could ask Pooch to sing and they think that, for their sake, she would probably rouse herself to do it, but even the most degenerated among them knows better than to mention it, except for Mary Ann, whom they keep shushing and who keeps answering with yet another quack of "I forgot, I forgot."

★　★　★

The next day others enter the laboratory one by one, but each returns on her own two or four feet. Some are quite stuffed with cupcakes and fortune cookies. Some have been patted on the head and tickled under the chin or even given little kisses on the cheek. Clearly the doctor is using every means at his disposal. Many have eaten their fortunes, especially those who have forgotten how to read, but others have the little slips of paper tucked in the pockets of their sterilized blue smocks. Many of the fortunes read more like warnings, though not all:

Continue on your present course and you will never be
an intellectual.
You will figure prominently in the nightmares of others.
You will never marry a prince. To be a duck is to marry a
duck.
Beware of changes that do not foster motherhood.

And so forth.

* * *

None of the others return from the laboratory in anywhere near as bad shape as Pooch and Basenji. Some, in fact, even return with secret little smiles on their faces and, besides the fortunes, they have little gifts such as earrings, multicolored beads, and perfume, all from the five and ten. Some even have key rings with their number in gold paint on green or blue plastic. It almost suggests that the keys to the cages or to the laboratory itself might be the next reward. Some have a few red, white, or blue chits, but they can't figure out what to do with them except play checkers or tiddledywinks, which they do.

Through all this coming and going and through all the arguments as to whether the gifts should be accepted at all or, once accepted, used, and whether one *should* return with a smile on one's face, or whether one should be *allowed* to return with a smile, Pooch and Basenji have been absolutely silent. Pooch has been up and about in a kind of fit of dusting and sweeping, though flinching at the slightest touch or loud noise. She has cared for Basenji by herself, fed her and washed her (rather vigorously), but neither of them has uttered a sound, not even a whimper. Once or twice the baby has reached for Pooch, but after a good look at her it pulls away shouting its one word, "No."

Phillip has kept quiet through all this also, sitting in a lotus position and rocking back and forth, tongue flicking in and out between her teeth more than ever. She has not yet had her turn in the laboratory, but she is determined that, when the time comes, she will not be like the others, so easily daunted or so easily pleased. She will protest in no uncertain terms the treatment of all of them and especially the treatment of Basenji and Pooch. She resolves that, if need be, she will fight back, will grab hold and squeeze, will bite. She is thinking how wonderful if only she really were what she imitates so colorfully . . . how wonderful if she did have a bite that was deadly. But now, in her present form, she hasn't much more strength than an ordinary woman and the doctor is a tall, not at all fat, but large-boned man. She will have to be quick about it and get a good grip first. She also resolves that, if killing is necessary, she will not be turned away from it by any moral or tender feelings she has picked up from Pooch. Perhaps she can save them all.

As it happens, it is the doctor who is the quicker. He has her head in a noose on the end of a pole before she can get near him. He bought the noose especially for her, anticipating what he had to deal with and, though he knows by the cut of her jaw that she isn't poisonous, he isn't taking any chances. "Ah ha!" the doctor says, having seen her quick motion toward him. He cattle-prods her into the cage, releases her from the pole, and there she is, in spite of all her resolutions.

But she is determined to fight him any way she can. "Don't bother with a cookie," she says, her tongue refusing to behave as she wishes it to. She is trying to avoid all *esses* for the sake of dignity. "I'm on a diet, and anyway I don't play *little* game." But the doctor turns on the electricity on the side of the cage where she stands. After a few seconds of frantic twirling about, she discovers the turned-off side of the cage.

"Very good," the doctor says, "just four point four seconds." But then he reverses the current to the side where she is and she jumps back to the first part of the cage, then back and forth and back and forth, the doctor laughing at her and shouting, "Very good. Very, very good. And now, on the contrary, you *will* play a little game. *My* little game. Why this frantic effort to incorporate all the characteristics of a human being, though I must say you've hardly managed half of them? You should know, and I quote: 'The whole earth itself is no more than the puniest dot.'"

"Not to me."

Shock.

"Say it. Puny dot, puny dot. How can you understand anything if you don't know that?"

"It'th not."

Shock.

"If you understood the universe, which even itself may be a puny dot and in which the earth may be but a punier one, you would tell me everything you know and let me help to bring things back the way they should be — to this minor planet."

"Not to me it ithn't."

"Is!" The doctor is shouting and changing dials and pushing buttons as fast as he can. He is turning both sides on alternately and Phillip is skipping about from cage right to cage left in a grotesque dance. Ice water from a nozzle on the ceiling sprays on her head. Then the doctor turns on both sides at once. This lasts eight seconds.

"Stop! Stop! It ith a puny dot. I admit it."

Immediately the shocks stop and a chocolate-frosted cupcake pops out from the dispenser at the side.

"Five minutes," the doctor says, "from the beginning," and writes that down.

Phillip, in a sudden careless rage, throws the cupcake at him and is satisfied to see chocolate smudges on his white lab coat, but she is again subjected to the dance from side to side and then both sides. No place to go . . . but up! Phillip is an excellent climber. Up she goes until she's hanging, mostly from the top bars in a far corner of the cage. The shocks don't reach her there.

At first the doctor pokes at her with the stick he used to bring her in, but it's not long enough. Suddenly he seems very, very calm. "Well, well," he says, looking at his watch, "I believe it's already time for lunch. I want you to know I'm not at all put out. I am simply asking myself, can the world exist without ignorant and obstructive people such as you? And I answer myself that, of course it can't, so no sense in getting upset."

She's better at hanging on than he thinks, but still it's hard. By the time he comes back half an hour later, Phillip's fingers and toes are so stiff and cramped she can neither hang on any longer nor let go.

"I suppose you're ready to come down?"

A meek "Yeth."

"Try it. I might have had it turned off all along. I'm not an ogre, you know. I only want what's best for all of us, you included. Think how much better you'd feel if you were back in some rain forest or other — or is it the desert? I can arrange for that. Just tell me the information I need to be able to help us all out of this awful mess."

It's true, Phillip has sometimes had vague yearnings toward life in the wild, though she knows very little about it and has never actually been in a forest, having been born in a pet shop.

"So now perhaps we understand each other better and can be of help to each other," the doctor says, "and I trust that, if and when you get a cupcake, you will eat it. So let us go on to another question. Tell me, who is your leader?"

"A little old lady who liveth in thith area, actually, who always wears navy blue or gray." Phillip, rubbing her sore fingers, begins a lengthy description of the doctor's wife, as minute as she can make it in order to gain time, but adding several characteristics of a tiger. "Even," she says, "striped already on the face. You can thee the orange, white, and black. Quite attractive." (Actually, Phillip is thinking of her own attractive red, black, and yellow.) "But more like a tiger every day and already quite dangerouth. I would stay away from her if I were you. In fact, she'd tear you limb from limb." Phillip says this last with relish.

"Females are all such liars," the doctor says. "Lies, that's all I've heard from all of you starting with little number 106 who hardly spoke at all. But then," and he quotes, "'Nobody is surprised when a fig tree brings forth figs.'" He gives Phillip another forced dance from side to side and soon she is climbing the wall of the cage again in spite of her sore toes and fingers.

"Watch out," the doctor says, "or I'll leave you here again with the floor turned on full and I won't come back until tomorrow."

Phillip, exhausted from the pain of the shocks and of her cramped hands and feet and of the leaping about, drops back down in a dejected coil that the doctor finds quite seductive, partly because of its submissiveness. The floor is, thank goodness, turned off.

"There are no leaderth that I know of," she says. "If there are, no one has told me about them. And I don't know how all thith thtarted. I just began to take such pleathure in my own body. It was thtrange. And I began to realize things. Most of all to know I wath alive. Alive! That'th all I thought about at first, even after that time the rocking chair rocked on me and no one seemed to care. And I don't know how all thith came about but it seemed such a privilege. I was . . . suddenly so . . . joyful!"

Another series of shocks, side to side and side to side, until Phillip climbs the mesh bars again. "Alligatorth," she shouts. "They have come out of the sewers." (Little does she realize how right she is. It's true. They *have* come up, though with no plans.) "Alligators all over the place and we have joined them. It'th their fault."

Two cupcakes, two fortune cookies, and three chits pop out. Also a string of large blue beads, and the doctor writes down the one word, ALLIGATORS, with exclamation point.

"You may go," he says. "Take your things and go, and I must say you've utterly worn me out, but in the end you did well. I'll be having another discussion with you soon. Very soon."

Later on when she reads her fortunes, one says "Consider practical alternatives," and the other "You will soon fall in love with a much older man." From the very beginning, the doctor has been quite taken with her.

CHAPTER VI
A Sorrowful Leave-Taking

The malice of a good thing is the barb
that makes it stick.

Richard Brinsley Sheridan

Basenji no sooner seems to be making some slight recovery than
the doctor comes for her again. His policy is to come for them
before they are let out of their cages in the morning in order to
avoid mass uprising. It's a good thing, because now that he has
come for Basenji there surely would have been a spontaneous
mutiny. Though Basenji is utterly limp and passive, all the others
(except for Pooch, who lies on her back, arms folded across her
chest, feet in the air, face partly covered by one golden ear) are
frantic. They bang on the bars and call out, "No, not Basenji!"
and, "Take me instead. I'll go. I'll say anything you want me to."
Of course it must be remembered that some of them have had
quite a pleasant experience in the laboratory — only a few mild
shocks and several treats and trinkets. And some would be only
too happy to go, simply to add variety to their days though they,
of course, are the ones who have not been treated to the worst of
what the doctor can do. Some, as mentioned, have even found
the doctor fascinating, his long, sad face quite appealing and
handsome if you like that type. And, though they dare not
confess it to the others, if their fortunes have mentioned a tall,
dark stranger, most (as he intended they should) have taken it to
mean the doctor himself, even though he is less black-haired
than gray. They are thinking of their own desirability in contrast
to his dumpy old wife and they are hoping for a meaningful
relationship — almost any kind of relationship, even if it is somewhat sadistic.

48

There are some, quite a few in fact, who had been beaten by their masters or even their fathers when young, and who nearly swooned with pleasure at the treatment they received in the laboratory as long as it didn't become *too* painful, and who enjoyed being the center of attention in whatever manner and for whatever reason. Their concern for Basenji is nonetheless genuine.

The doctor had brought cattle prod, handcuffs, and muzzle when coming for Basenji, but there is no need. She lies in his arms, eyes shut, face expressionless, serene actually. All are so taken by her ethereal beauty and her youth that they stop their clamoring. The doctor and Basenji seem to form a sort of reverse Pietà, the doctor holding her gently and looking a bit compassionate, and Basenji, one graceful, slender limb dangling and the other, as though in modesty, lying across her just barely budding breasts, which are clearly outlined by the folds of the blue smock as it drapes around her.

Phillip is suddenly very afraid for her. "Fight back," she yells. "Don't let go. Pleath don't let go." She is also thinking that Basenji, with one good surprise bite in the right place . . . and, in truth, Basenji's mouth is lying against the doctor's jugular vein. *She* is the one who could save them all. "Right now! Bite!" Phillip screams, but it's no use. Basenji, in her present condition, can no more bite than could a wet rag. And she doesn't come back. They wait for her the whole day, wondering about her and wondering what to do for her when she comes, but she never does, not that day and not the next either.

They decide to hold a little nondenominational memorial service for her just in case she is no more. They all feel it is too much to hope for that she has been released or is alive somewhere else in the house. They ask Rosemary for candles and flowers and she, always accommodating when she can be, brings them six white candles and more than enough flowers from her own garden. Her choices make everyone think that she must have had Basenji specifically in mind: white daisies, small purple irises, miniature tulips delicately colored yellow in the centers and pink at the edges. They are telling each other that, had

Basenji chosen to be a flower, certainly she would have chosen to be one of these.

Of course they ask Pooch if she will sing. This they want most of all. But she, shaking her head no, and still not speaking, only gives a harsh breathy cough, almost as though that were the only sound she is capable of making. They do not press her, but ask if, instead, she might write a few words or a poem. This she consents to do. Yes, she tells herself, she must rouse herself. She really must. For Basenji's sake, even though, of course, no one knows for sure if she is really dead or not, but chances are, considering the condition she was in, that she is. Yes, and Pooch knows that she herself would be capable of such a death . . . just lie down and give up. Perhaps if it wasn't for the baby and for the others whom she might be able to help later on, who knows but that she, too, would . . . will. . . .

As to the few words that she must have ready the next day, she remembers some lines from Olaf Stapledon in which the great dog, Sirius himself, thinks, "A poem might be sincere no matter how hastily it had been scribbled," and she begins work on one. She is thinking, if only she could stop this twitching and trembling and if only her mind didn't dart about as though avoiding . . . particularly avoiding thoughts of Basenji and of the laboratory, and if only she didn't feel so drained.

And how she would love to talk to the psychotherapist again. What would he tell her to do to cope with these problems? To cope with her own feelings? Perhaps there is rage underneath all this. How not use it against herself? And what about her beloved master! Has Isabel already taken her place in his heart? If only she knew that she would see him once again, there would be something to look forward to.

But poor Basenji! What trials has she had to bear? Even before all this began, she and Basenji had, the second evening, leaning their heads together against their cage bars, whispered to each other their past histories and all their secrets (though Pooch has no real secrets to tell), so Pooch knows that Basenji, of all creatures, could not possibly have known anything about any conspiracy or any leaders. Pooch probably *should* have known, and therefore in some way deserves the "punishment" she is getting for her ignorance — though actually they all seem ignorant, even Phillip — but what could Basenji have been expected to know? Why, she grew up in a top-floor apartment, never once having ventured down the elevator, let alone out into the street. That is, until that one night. And then so frightened by the honking, the lights, and the rain that she ran and didn't stop until she was completely exhausted and lost. They had been, Basenji had said, about to go on a trip to Europe. That she knew. And somehow (how, even Basenji herself could never figure out) she had slipped out of her brand-new harness and fled. At the time, for her master's pleasure (her master was eleven years old) she had been dressed *"à l'oriental."* This had almost gotten her into much more trouble in the streets until she had the presence of mind to remove the embroidered slippers and the voluminous red trousers which, in the pouring rain, had become quite draggled. The green satin shirt, without the yellow vest, served as a sort of minidress and did not attract so much attention. She had, she confessed, frequently been involved in sexual play with her young master, but not going "all the way," so to speak, and so still technically a virgin in spite of all they had known of each other. However, Basenji said, she had known that "all the way" must come soon, and she dreaded it. This was a side of Basenji that only Pooch knew and, of course, would never tell. Whatever poor Basenji's life had been, Pooch knew it was certainly not her fault. The poor thing had just barely reached adolescence and now, to be cut down at first flowering, never to know true love and a true loving sexuality. To Pooch, Basenji would always be the essence of the sweet and the virginal. And how sad that, at this very moment, her owners were probably enjoying Paris while Basenji, *pauvre petite,* would never see it.

She wishes that she had more time to write the poem, that it could be better, not for her own pride, but for Basenji's sake. She wants to do the absolute best that she can in this last task for her friend. As it is, she finishes it just in time for the service, which is very moving and beautiful, though everyone wishes that Pooch, rather than writing about songs, had sung.

Poem on the Death of a Dear Dear Friend

First crocus of the season
Whiter than the very snow
I have watched it tremble
When the harsh winds blow

This spring, though it come not again,
Will linger ever in mind
As will the crocus. Another one so white
And pure I will not find.

I would lift my voice in song
And let the bleak wind hear my cries
But hope the crocus doth sleep on,
For her my voice be lullabies.

Pooch hopes that someday, especially if they do not live through this experience, someone might set the poem to music, and Basenji thereby be remembered.

CHAPTER VII
In Which the Baby Learns
a Second Word

None are so bold as the timid, when
they are fairly roused.

Elizabeth Barrett

Now the doctor is going to try a completely new direction. He
brings into the laboratory a solid Morris chair and arranges
leather straps as though to confine the individual in it, but he
cuts them all partway through. The thick one for the waist he will
not even buckle, but will let it hang out the back of its own
weight. Of course he must be careful not to let 107 realize that
she's not strapped in except lightly at wrist and elbow.

He opens one of the high little basement windows. Takes out
the thick screening that serves as bars. Only someone quite at the
end of her rope could make such a leap up from the floor to what
she would take as freedom. Even then, probably impossible. Still,
can't be guessed at, what they can or can't do. Not to take any
chances, the doctor places a small stool and then a waist-high
bookcase next to it to form steps. Then he adjusts the testing cage
so that it gives only the slightest of shocks even when turned on
full. Partly this is in case he gets carried away. It's possible that he
might get very angry. Often does these days. He's found out so
little so far. Suspects most of them are as ignorant as they say they
are. But not 108 and 107. They know things. And something wise
about them that the others respect. They're listened to. 107 may
lead him somewhere useful. Perhaps to their leader. Except she
doesn't talk now. Could tell that from the tapes. *There's* a waste of
time. All those tapes. Grunts, chuckles, quacks. Even worse than
it used to be. Bad enough then. Bla, bla, bla. "How do I look with
feathers in my ears?" "Tell me, is my topknot mostly blue or

green?" "Have my feet grown ugly already?" "Am I too fat? Too thin?" Pleasant singing voice, though, 107's was. Powerful. A bit strange. Music. Used to like it. Beethoven. What they say about menstrual and estrous might be useful. Somewhat. Try to find their most vulnerable times of the month or year as the case may be. Some of them in love with me. Should use that, too. 108. What was her name? What about Rosemary? Eyes sometimes little slits. Watching. Did she do that before? Not when first married. Eyes wide then. Blue. Or were they gray? And she's not done some things lately. Noticed dust. Everything done for *them*, though. Last night thought to try love-making again, but it's been a long time. How to begin after. . . . Is it years? Tired. Thought better of it. 108 didn't fool me with that tiger bit. No stripes on Rosemary. Though hunched up and gained a little weight. 108 a bit thin. Long. Quite attractive. She and 107 team? Go where there is an answer. Not sit around here any more. Put running shoes on. Lunchbox, sweater, raincoat by the door. Get started. First the baby.

★   ★   ★

There is, of course, quite a row when the doctor takes the baby. More so even than for Basenji (especially now that Basenji has not returned). Phillip had the baby in her cage as usual, and she let it go to the doctor's arms willingly enough, thinking that it was she he had come for, but then she was pushed back roughly into her cage and the baby was taken. What a commotion as the doctor leaves with it! Such caterwaulings, from throaty croak to skirr. The doctor distinctly heard one dreadful raucous yawp from 107. Quite distasteful and quite unlike her usual voice. He is thinking that she sounds exactly like what her reputation (Isabel's) made him think she would sound like in the first place.

He decides to wait until they have all tired themselves out a bit before coming back for number 107. Let them get it off their chests. It's quite unpleasant to be exposed to it even for a few seconds. And what are they thinking, letting the baby hear such a racket! Meanwhile examine it. Cute little thing. Too bad never had one of his own. He puts it on the floor and lets it crawl around and play with the paraphernalia in the room. It looks healthy. Seems to be doing all right on kibbles and cat food. "Bop," it says, "Bop, bop." The doctor is pleased, thinking it might be trying to say "Pop." He makes up little experiments for the baby, measuring how fast it can crawl and how long its attention span is. Also what kind of things motivate it the most to pay attention or to crawl. Twice he gives it a little pinch. Not enough to make it cry, only to protest. In such a manner he passes a pleasant three-quarters of an hour, finally putting the baby in the testing cage (making sure it's only loosely latched) and going back for 107. They are all, by that time, and thank goodness, so hoarse they can hardly do more than whisper their protests. He doesn't say a word. All the better if they think that dreadful things are happening to the baby.

Of course Pooch comes willingly enough. It is obvious that she can hardly wait to get to the laboratory to see what's going on with the baby, and it's also obvious that she is horrified to find it in the testing cage.

The doctor straps Pooch into the chair. "Let's see how fast the baby learns which side of the cage is which," he says, and, "Of course you can stop this any time you want to."

Pooch opens her mouth, but only strange croaking sounds come out.

"In that case. . . ." the doctor says, and gives the first shock.

"Ouch," the baby says, perfectly clearly and rather gravely, "Ouch, ouch, ouch." Under other circumstances Pooch would have been delighted with the new word. Now she is all the more distressed by it and by the nature of the new word itself and by the serious way it has been spoken. After a few moments of skittering around and saying "Ouch," the baby finds the safe side of the cage.

"Not bad," the doctor says. "Actually better than some. Now let's try it the other way round."

This goes on, the doctor increasing the shocks by infinitesimal intervals, hoping soon to find the precise level at which the baby will begin to cry. He hopes, then, to be able to turn the crying on and off by the push of a button. Meanwhile Pooch continuously makes that funny, throaty sound. It is only when the baby is quite suddenly crying vigorously with hurt and frustration, tired of the game, not stopping even with the shocks completely turned off, and when Pooch is almost through the already cut straps, that the doctor suddenly realizes: My God, 107! She's barking!

At that moment Pooch is full of such mixed feelings she doesn't know what she will do. Her teeth have never once been used, even when she was a baby, for anything more savage than pulling on a rag or chewing an old shoe, but now she must . . . yes, it is the only answer. Besides, when she thinks of what has happened to her voice, that she would have died for, and that she would also willingly die for the baby. . . . And what's to lose, when she already has Isabel's reputation? Loyalty is a trap, she thinks, and the doctor has saved us only for torture and death as with poor Basenji. Attack, then. The throat, the shoulder. She had not known she had such strength, the bonds broken already, and so easily! The doctor on the floor, Pooch doesn't stop to see if he's dead or alive. She pushes the latch of the testing cage, grasps the baby in her teeth, and, ignoring the system of steps put out for her, she makes that extraordinary leap up to and through the open basement window, the baby shouting, "No, no, no, no," at the top of its voice.

CHAPTER VIII
Escamillo!

> The more they sink, the more fervently
> glow their eyes. . . .
> *Friedrich Nietzsche*

At the moment there are several murderers at large. One of them is Isabel (the real Isabel). She had come close to murder several times before, as might be guessed. And she has maimed, though never so seriously that the victim couldn't be rehabilitated and function almost at his former level. Some of these episodes happened before she had even remotely come to resemble a wolverine. But now she *has* killed and has taken off toward Central Park in hope of escape even though she is, in her present state, only vaguely aware of the magnitude of her crime and therefore probably could not be punished for it should it ever come to trial. (It could easily be proved, however, that Pooch understands at all times what she is doing.)

Considering the situation, it is actually surprising that there haven't been more murders and more serious maimings. Several of the misadventures that have occurred were clearly inadvertent, the creatures not realizing their own strength or the sharpness of their teeth and claws. They were as horrified as anyone to find the damage they had done. Of course this is not always the case, for there are those, like Isabel, who have never been particularly gentle individuals and who are very pleased with their new-found fiercenesses.

As one might surmise, while Isabel did get to the Plaza, she did not stay there long. At the first sight of her, two large men in uniforms with gold braid asked her to leave, and no small wonder. Isabel was looking quite disreputable, trailing wood chips, and although her hair is short and fits around her head like a little black cap, it had been neither combed nor washed for days and stuck out in clumps in several directions. She had long ago discarded her silver high-heeled shoes as too confining and was now comfortably barefoot. There were vestiges of heavy makeup smeared about her face, the black from around her eyes having somehow gotten around her mouth and the red from her lips having somehow gotten around her eyes.

"Is good," Isabel told the two uniformed men. "Fine. Find. Must meet. One. Or two men."

Hearing her guttural, garbled speech, the men grabbed her and tried to push her out, but she broke free and raced around the lobby knocking over people and furniture quite like the animal that she most resembles. Then she made a dash through the dining room and out into the kitchen where a cook had a large tenderloin he was just about to cut into tournedos. The sight was too much for Isabel, who was sick of a whole week's worth of meals of dry dog food. She went utterly berserk. Killed the sauce man, who had come to the aid of the cook, and maimed the cook, who had made the mistake of trying to rescue his tenderloin from the half-woman, half-animal trying to make off with it.

Of course it did not take the police detective long to find out that the murderer is either: (a) a creature named Isabel, or (b) a creature named Pooch, both recently released from the pound. One of them said to be degenerating rapidly and the other said to possess a youthful shyness, but who knows what violence may lurk beneath a maidenly reticence. The detective will not allow himself to be misled by surfaces.

★ ★ ★

And now Pooch, out into the sunny spring morning, running as fast as she can, and does not stop until completely out of breath, then, panting, slows to a dog-trot. The almost superhuman strength that she has felt ever since the need arose to rescue the baby seems now to be waning. She finally slows to a walk. Then stops. Then hides next to the stairway of a brownstone and tries to make herself and the baby a bit more presentable. She is shaking all over and there are tears in her eyes. She wipes off . . . or rather, rubs off the dried stains as best she can and hides them a bit by wearing her smock wrong side out. (Odd, they do not *smell* like blood.) She removes and throws away the baby's torn vest. Thank God it's warm enough. Only now, in this breathing space, does she realize how cut and bruised her feet are, for they had not been allowed shoes. Probably to make it harder to run away.

As she is busy cleaning herself as best she can, she suddenly realizes that she has, all this time, been hearing a strange clop-clopping sound like hundreds . . . thousands of high-heeled shoes, and grunts, and a kind of lowing. It seems to be coming from the end of the block. Something is happening, something big. It raises the hair on the back of her neck, though she doesn't know why. She steps out into the street to try to see down the block. There are brownish creatures heading north, trotting down the middle of the far avenue. Pooch is thinking, what a wonderful place to hide! To go with them, in the center, hidden by their bodies! She hurries to the corner and finds them even more impressive than she had first thought, a huge herd, thousands of them, all up and down Third Avenue as far as one can see (for Pooch has already run all the way from the Upper West Side to the Lower East). Many have colorful backpacks or rolled-up yellow or red raincoats slung over their shoulders. Some have wide-brimmed hats. All have large paper or plastic bags that obviously contain their meals for several days, and all are trotting by at a fairly fast clip, clopping in their clogs or teetering in their high-heeled pumps, some still upright, others on all fours. Cars are honking at them from the side streets, mounted police are trying to disrupt them or change their course, but to no avail. As soon as the police manage to cut off a small group, they break free again and rejoin the herd.

Pooch wonders for a moment about the policemen's horses, seeming to see on the face of one of them (mild brown eyes and long platinum mane) the look of a woman, but then she notices, shyly taking modest glances, that they all seem to be males. (Of course they are geldings, but Pooch knows nothing of such things.) She has heard about horses pulling carts or being ridden, but has not seen any before. She finds them so sensitive looking and aristocratic that she wonders how they can allow themselves to be demeaned in this manner. She supposes they have, in spite of their noble looks and large size, low opinions of their own worth just as the psychologist said she had. Perhaps later on, when and if the world ever really does get straightened out and there is a complete redistribution of power and, especially, profits, they can afford to get the psychological help they need and learn to be more assertive.

She turns again to the migrating herd. If only they would take her along, hide her in their midst, she and the baby might yet be saved! For it is clear that they are going on a very long journey, and nothing could be better right now for Pooch and baby. She hurries up to them, silently mouthing the words *help* and *please*. (In all this clatter they'd not have heard her even if she could speak out.) But they pay her no attention, seem to have eyes and grunts only for each other. One of them steps with a sharp spiked heel on Pooch's bare toe when Pooch gets too close. She lets out a yelp, then limps on. Mustn't stop now when safety for her and the baby may be so near. Of course there's no way she can tell one of them her troubles. She can only whimper and bark and groan and in all this clopping and lowing and grunting they can't (or won't) hear her. The one or two who do notice her say, though they are not particularly bovine in appearance, "Moooooove, moooooove," and in no uncertain terms. One says, "Goooooooww," and that is clear, too, but Pooch thinks, are they not sisters? Are we not in this together? It seems not. Pooch holds the baby up to them as beseechingly as she can, letting tears come to her eyes, tears that were close anyway, but to no avail. If only she could really speak to them. Surely they are not as hard-hearted as they seem. But now one of them has deliberately knocked her down. Pooch manages to fall so that she scrapes her elbows rather than letting any harm come to the baby, who, thank goodness, laughs at the misadventure and says another "Ouch."

Then Pooch's tears really come. For a moment it all seems so unfair, even that she should be burdened with this baby that laughs when Pooch hurts herself. But then the little creature turns to her with a dazzling smile and says softly, "No, no, no." Pooch kisses its warm cheeks and her courage returns. She will watch the herd for breaks and she will try to cross the street. It may be safer on the other side. As she watches, she realizes that it would probably have been quite dangerous to the baby and to herself, the blind way these creatures are running, to try to run in their midst. Probably utterly ruin her feet. Perhaps the one who pushed her deliberately was really doing her a favor. She notices that some of them are quite out of breath, but it's clear that they do not dare to drop out. Others bump into them from behind, that's what all the grunting is about. They shove each other along; it's quite brutal. No, better that she should cross the street when she can and head away from them. This she manages to do after waiting several minutes and seeing the herd thin out a bit.

She limps south. She feels a bit safer on this side of the herd, but of course one can't be sure. She tries to keep away from the mounted police, though they pay not the slightest attention to her in spite of her skimpy smock and bare bruised feet. But then, they are probably used to any sort of dress or undress these days. It would take a lot to surprise them.

Suddenly Pooch hears the sound of music coming from quite nearby. Opera! How could she not have noticed it before, in spite of the racket in the street, for here is a wonderful baritone voice and the familiar words coming from a small building, the stage door open. *"Le cirque est plein de sang! On se sauve, on franchit les grilles! C'est ton tour maintenant! Allons! . . ."* Allons indeed! She cannot resist it. But such a small theater! Pooch creeps in, finds herself backstage in the wings, and hides behind a packing box. Yes, yes, it's he, tall, broad-shouldered, black hair and black mustache, and dressed all in silver and black! Surely, she thinks, this is what love is all about, true, true love, the drums beating. Will she dare to make a gesture in his direction? Will she dare to look him in the eye? She cannot speak, but perhaps a little moan of appreciation would not be inappropriate. Of course it's to be expected that one so bold and so darkly handsome will have many lovers. She must accept that. She will. She will forgive him anything.

Pooch settles back to watch and listen. The trembling and twitching that have been with her since her first visit to the laboratory finally stop and she forgets her troubles, fascinated by the dark man who is in such control of himself and others and listening to the music that she has always loved the best of all.

It's a dress rehearsal. Arias are stopped in the middle sometimes and some of the movement on stage is changed. It is all fascinating to Pooch, though she does wish she could hear the arias through to the end, especially her favorites. All the females have voices of somewhat unusual timbre. Clearly a high C means very little to some of them. They could go on up another octave and perhaps on up into the range that only such as Pooch can hear.

After she has watched and rested for an hour she notices near her a cardboard box full of costumes. In fact it looks rather like old, discarded bits of costumes. If it didn't look as though it were about to be thrown out, Pooch could not have brought herself to touch it, even though she knows that she really must find other clothes. Rummaging through it, she is delighted to find the makings of a wonderful kind of gypsy outfit, quite the fashion, too: long skirt, scarves, beads, all needing some repair. The beads are half unstrung, but Pooch fixes several strands of them that are still hanging together fairly well. Then she dresses herself and the baby to match. She's sure she looks quite a different person, bandana round her head, gold-fringed scarf and fringed skirt, dangly earrings for her silky ears. And she has found sandals to protect her poor bruised feet. Never in her life has she had such finery as this. She feels, for the first time, that she might be, perhaps, a little bit attractive. Perhaps she *will* dare to smile at the dark and handsome baritone. Yes, she will. She promises herself that she will make some gesture toward him that is even more than just a smile.

All this has taken quite a long time, and now the rehearsal is over. The singers have gone to change out of their costumes and there are too many people roaming about backstage for Pooch to feel safe there, even behind the large packing box, so she hurries outside, but waits by the stage door. She feels quite happy and excited and *so* well dressed. If only her voice would return to her, just for two or three well-chosen words, she could not ask for more. What with the loss of Basenji and the danger to the baby, as well as to all the others, she has not really thought that much about the loss of her voice. It seems such an insignificant thing when lives are lost or in danger, but hearing the singing has brought pangs of regret so strong that Pooch feels she could hardly breathe, and now . . . now especially she does so need to speak.

The herd has all gone by, though now and then Pooch sees a straggler, on the sidewalk this time, clop-clopping north, high heels, backpack, bundles, and a worried expression on her face. Pooch is thinking that, if a conspiracy exists, as the doctor seemed to think, then maybe these are the conspirators, though they certainly are not secretive, and they seem to be lured on by something more primitive than an idea. Some deep inner urge. It's in their faces. And yet, Pooch wonders, does not some atavistic need exist in all of us to save the world, exactly to the degree that we would save ourselves, for aren't we "the world" as much as any other piece in it? Perhaps the more animal we are . . . that is, Pooch thinks, that I should keep my basic nature even while becoming (or, rather, hoping to become) an intellectual . . . if I could retain strong links to my animal past. Never forget what I am and where I come from. . . .

Meanwhile, people have been coming out the stage door and Pooch, in spite of her musings, has scrutinized each one carefully. But no dark, broad-shouldered man with mustache has appeared. It begins to grow dark. Finally it is clear that everyone has gone. It is then that Pooch has a sudden insight. What about that thin, blond, pale young man who smiled at her shyly? No mustache, no broad shoulders—but he's the only one it could have been! She remembers him clearly. She thought at the time he seemed quite sweet and she had even thought that he might help her, smiling at her as he did, but she was waiting for the glamorous . . . for the glittering . . . for Escamillo himself to walk out, no doubt to the sound of trumpets. So here she is, not having made a single gesture toward anyone though she had promised herself firmly that she would. And she had not even smiled back at that young man, looking, as she was, so intently for someone else . . . for the imaginary man, larger than life.

CHAPTER IX
Shocking Passions

> Thus far his errors had been abnormal,
> inhumanly perverted dallyings with the
> unspeakable.
>
> *John Taine*

Now come out the creatures that can see in the dark. Odd hunched-over beings, some of them with long heads and shining eyes. Half this, half that — it's hard to tell exactly what. Is it possible, Pooch wonders, seeing them, that we are as dangerous to each other as we seem to be to the more dominant sex? Are there such as Phillip, for example, but poisonous, now roaming these very streets? Why not? Pooch decides to keep an ear out for any ominous rattling sounds, and having thoughts about rattling brings her to rats. What about them? And what about those who are becoming rats? Perhaps that's who these gray figures are. There seems to be a devilish intelligence in their eyes. How to avoid them?

"Bop, bop?" the baby questions. Suddenly it's wide awake. "Bop, bop, bop? Littlely dittlely, littlely dittlely." Pooch tries to shush it. She certainly doesn't want to attract attention in this part of town and at this time of night.

Except for that evening at Lincoln Center, Pooch has never been on the streets of the city at such a late hour and certainly never in such a dingy area, full of indigent men who, in this weather, sleep in doorways, their empty beer cans beside them. The bag ladies, it seems, have all disappeared, gone on to worse or better things, slithering into the sewers or . . . well, perhaps these gray things *are* the bag ladies. Pooch wishes them every happiness possible in their new forms, but thinks that to sleep on the streets with these bright-eyed creatures roaming about seems

65

quite dangerous. But what else is there to do? She turns down a side street to see if she can find some hidden basement doorway that is not already occupied. She passes several long-legged things with boas who are standing under a streetlight at the next corner. They have blue or green short-cropped — Pooch isn't sure whether hair, hats, or feathers — and large black areas around their eyes. It might be makeup, but it might be the way their eyes really are. They seem angry with her for coming near them and whistle their warnings. The baby, delighted with the colorful creatures, reaches toward one of them and calls out, "Littlely dittlely," but the creature turns as if to peck it. Pooch is horrified to find herself giving a warning bark. It works, though. They hurry back into the shadows. Pooch trots away and a few minutes later she does find a secluded basement doorway. There she settles down to watch until morning, hoping that she can stay awake to guard the baby.

If only there really was a conspiracy, she thinks, but as far as she can tell there isn't. But if no one is in charge of all this, then perhaps someone *should* be. Perhaps she herself, inexperienced as she is. . . . A vast network could be formed, she is not sure for what purpose. Perhaps self-protection, or to help things along, though of course Mother Nature has always done fairly well on her own with only a modicum of help from human beings (or perhaps one should call it hindrance). In almost all cases Nature seems to know what she is doing, except, of course, where tail feathers are too long for decent flight or, as in the sex life of the snail, with its sex organs on its head and, one might say, a bit excessive in its passions, though Pooch, never having experienced such things as yet, realizes that she should not be judgmental of other creatures when she knows so little about it. Yes, perhaps they could all help Nature along a bit, or at least help to find some order in this chaos.

But perhaps it isn't chaos at all. Just seems so. If only she hadn't lost her voice! And now, again, the enormity of her loss hits her. Not to sing! Perhaps never to sing again, let alone speak! Perhaps only to croak like a frog. No, no, she must admit it's barking. How could she have let herself regress so after all her hard work to be both human and humane? So the worst has already happened. This is certainly, if not the, then *one* of the fates-worse-than-death that she has heard about. Well, nothing for it but to go on. The baby needs her. Her friends back at the doctor's need her, for she is the only one on the outside who can help them. Does the world need her? Only if she makes that true by doing the best she can for it. And what about that slim tan-eyed young man? Good she did not try to relate to him. He would have been shocked at the sounds she might have made. She must be careful to keep her mouth shut from now on. That last bark was quite inadvertent. What a silly fool she was not to know better than to fall in love with an image. Hasn't she read that all romantic love is like that? A sort of mistake? Nice smile, though, there by the door. Very nice smile. And with that thought she dozes off in spite of herself.

★   ★   ★

"Nice ass."

"Nice tits, too. I'd like to see more of 'em."

"Want to sleep with me, sweetie?"

"Sure she do. Man, you got the biggest."

"Yeah. Show her."

"Let her alone. She don't fuck around."

"All the better. I like the fucking ones that don't fuck around."

"Why don't she say nothin'?"

"If it ain't no, it's gotta be yes."

"She no cherry. She got a baby."

"Hey, gimme that fucking baby."

"Bop, bop?" it says, and then what sounds like, "Later, later."

"Lady, let me see them tits." He pulls at her blouse, popping off the top buttons.

"She no lady."

"If that baby's a girl we could help it along some."

Pooch, who has been backed into a corner by the basement door, suddenly lunges forward, pulling her lips back from teeth and letting out a series of fierce growls, roars, and barks, all combined one with the other. The three boys turn and try to scramble up the stairs at the same time. Pooch rips the pants of one of them and pulls the shoe off another, drawing blood in the process, though not much. She is, even right in the middle of it all, horrified with herself. Twice now she has behaved like a dangerous animal. There must be much of the she-wolf in her. More than she ever suspected. Certainly she deserves to have Isabel's reputation, more's the pity.

If only she were religious, she might pray for guidance and have someone to ask forgiveness from besides her master and the psychologist. Or if only they were here. And how sad to be so far from home. But she must not forget the operas, the wonderful operas, the big one that first night and the little one today . . . yesterday, that is. Those memories will remain forever a comfort to her. Had she not suffered the trials of these last weeks, she certainly would not have had those joys, nor the joy of meeting so many new friends, nor would she have had the opportunity of easing poor Basenji's pain in whatever way she could. And the baby! Perhaps it is alive today because of her, for the mistress might have done much more harm to it later on and Pooch might not have been able to defend it. But then again, she herself is fiercer than she ever thought she was. Perhaps that's just as well. She turns and covers the baby's face with kisses as though to prove that she indeed still has a soft heart.

Just then a bright light goes on right over her head. It turns out that this is not the door to a basement, but to a basement apartment, and someone is looking out the heavily barred window at her. She can see big, suspicious black eyes and a big, black, Escamillo sort of mustache, though the face it is attached to seems a bit too pudgy. No, the mustache is larger than any Escamillo would have and curls up at the sides. The eyes are Italian, the mouth that of a voluptuary. Surely, Pooch thinks, this is the face of an opera lover like herself. Surely she has been lucky in her choice of basement doorways.

Behind the bars, Pooch sees that the window is open. She gestures toward the baby and then gives what she hopes is a graceful little bow not unlike what she saw at the end of the acts at the New York City Opera. She wants to say, "Kind Sir. Kind, kind, kind Sir," or words to that effect. This is the first time since she lost her voice that she has actually tried to say, calmly, a few words, but all that comes out is a sort of yearning whine.

"Cut the bullshit." The voice is high for one so wide as he looks to be. "I heard you and I saw what you did. Now get out of my doorway. And you better not have peed down here."

Pooch hangs her head, nodding at the same time because, actually, she had, in the far corner (where else was there to go?) and she never, never lies, except about such things as complimenting other people's hats.

"Get out of here . . . bitch."

Blushing with shame even though, technically, she *is* a bitch, Pooch turns to gather up the baby and the rolled-up scarves she had been using for a pillow. She knows that one must remain philosophical about such harsh words. They are bound to come even to those with the best intentions and sometimes when one tries one's hardest to please, though of course this was not the case here since she didn't even know of the man's existence. Naturally, had she known this was his front door, she would have been more careful. If only she could speak and apologize, and perhaps if she could tell him what she's been through and what led to her spending the night in his doorway, he would be moved by her story and understand that she had had few choices. He might even take her in and serve her a good breakfast. (Pooch has not eaten for almost twenty-four hours, so this is on her mind.) But the way he said "bitch," and took such slow pleasure in making the word sound ugly . . . disgusting. . . . Naturally it's not the first time she has been called that, and she knows she shouldn't be insulted by the word since it's true, but they always mean to be insulting. She's heard them use the word *girl* the same way, telling some poor little boy that he's just like a girl, which, regardless of what he may think of girls, always makes him feel dreadful. If she could speak, perhaps this is the question to which she should address herself, not her own individual problems but this larger one, telling him that, while she *is* a bitch, she does not want the word used in a way that is demeaning to

herself and to other bitches like her and that the same goes for
the word *girl.*

Anyway I will leave here like an opera star, she thinks. She has
become quite angry about little boys being called girls as an
insult. The poor little fellows suffer so from it. One should not
allow it. (Pooch is always quick to anger at injustice to others,
though seldom rouses herself when it is she who is put upon.) In
her most regal manner, then, she starts up the stairs.

"Wait a minute."

The fat man has opened his door and is looking out at her. His
voice sounds quite different. All the shrillness has gone out of it.
Now it is low (more befitting his size) and seductive. It is clear
that he considers himself quite charming when he wants to be
and that, at least for the moment, he wants to be.

"You're no ordinary bitch, are you?" Now *bitch* means something entirely different, though again he dwells on the word.

And suddenly Pooch realizes the power of a pose. He has taken
her for what she has pretended to be these last few moments as
she started to climb the stairs. She turns, still in the role of prima
donna, and does not deign to answer even with a gesture. They
stand, looking at each other, Pooch forcing herself not to look
away. As she stares into his eyes, as soft and brown as her own, the
idea that she has killed a man comes to her, or rather that she has
probably killed one, and also that she has escaped a fortress. Even
though the doctor was probably a murderer himself, she feels
terrible about her crimes, and yet, if the circumstances warranted, she knows she would do such a thing again. And so she
does not look away. He, it is clear, is also bold. They cannot stare
each other down.

"Won't you come in," he says softly.

She is tempted to walk proudly away. Certainly she would
never consider going in except for the thought of food, especially
for the baby, and though he has not mentioned inviting her to
breakfast, she feels a tiny drop of drool at the corner of her
mouth. In order to keep up her dignified pose, she doesn't dare
lick it away. She hopes he hasn't noticed. She comes back down
the basement stairway as though entering a grand ballroom,

though she is inwardly laughing at herself and her notions of her own grandeur. And yet it seems to be working. She wonders how long she can keep up the pose.

Yes, it certainly is the apartment of a sybarite. Pooch, horrified, quickly covers the baby's eyes with her hand, but the baby protests to such a degree that there is nothing for it but that she take her hand away. The baby looks at everything with obvious delight. Clearly it has seen nothing that pleased it so much as these, the statues, the paintings, the paraphernalia (the uses of which Pooch has no idea), the doodads, large and small: pornographic candles, pornographic magnets, pornographic pillows on the sofa, pornographic lamp with pornographic shade, pornographic ash tray. . . . The baby crows out its whole repertoire, "No, ouch, bop, bop, littlely dittlely, later!" and proceeds to play an enthusiastic pattycake. Perhaps the baby in its turn will one day become a voluptuary.

The fat man, clearly delighted with the baby's delight, points out to Pooch the old-fashioned shepherd-shepherdess wallpaper with its little pornographic dramas going on from scene to scene, from bush to bush. "The original paintings from which these were copied," he tells her, "were made for Louis XVI. You must come and look at them more closely." He is all solicitude, his arm around her shoulders. "But, my dear, I imagine you're hungry. Why not study my wallpaper while I go and fix you a nice little steak?"

Perhaps he did see that bit of drool dripping down her chin. And now she can't help drooling even more than before, but she has not forgotten her vows. She shakes her head a vigorous *no* and then, keeping her dignity as best she can and also as gracefully as she can manage it, she pantomimes vegetables and nuts, first herself as carrot, then broccoli, then cashew nut, and finally she ends with herself as rain, the sun, shining down with a bright smile. Will he get the point? She gives a final little curtsy. He answers with a mocking bow. (Somehow he makes her feel operatic. No one has ever done that before except sometimes when she was singing.) "Then a salad it shall be," he says.

After he has moved out into the kitchen at the back, Pooch puts the baby on the floor and, keeping an eye on it, tries to find something to look at that's not pornographic. In a few minutes she finds a magazine that she has heard about but never seen before, *the Opera News*. It is on the little writing desk next to a pornographic eraser (worn down just "there"), and a pornographic pencil (two crocodiles entwined, each one's head to the other's tail). Pornography or not, Pooch thinks, how can he not but be a worthy person if he has this magazine, and she is immediately engrossed in it. She does not get far, however, before she sees a small ad:

Will the creature who sang out from the balcony on the night of May 14th please contact the impresario Valdoviccini at 555-6656 as soon as possible.

Pooch of course is instantly in tears. This, more than anything so far, brings home to her the disaster of the loss of her voice, but there is no time for self-pity. Luckily that name and telephone number are etched forever in her mind, for now she is interrupted by a shriek from the baby. Pooch lets out an unpremeditated little yelp which she stifles with her hand. At first she can't find the baby, but then she sees it crawling out from under the bed with four bloody scratches on its cheek. In the dark beyond it, under that huge, king-sized bed, she sees two luminous blue eyes.

"Pussy!"

The fat man has heard the commotion and is immediately down on his knees trying to poke the creature out with a large wooden spoon. "Pussy, you ungrateful wretch. Didn't I rescue you from several fates worse than death, as well as from death itself!"

"Out of the frying pan. . . ."

"Come out and behave yourself."

"Not until she and that other thing go."

"Don't be jealous. You were, yourself, not so long ago, in the very same situation as this young thing. Come out. We'll have a nice *ménage à trois*."

"It came after me."

"Don't be ridiculous. It's just a baby."

The spoon is evidently not long enough.

Pooch, watching it all and hardly realizing what she is doing, licks the blood from the baby's face. She stops herself in a moment and sees that there is really not much damage done, though there is always the risk of cat-scratch fever.

The fat man is flailing out quite violently now. By the wall at the far side of the bed appears a slinky, light tan (almost white, in fact) and almost black . . . a seal point, the blue eyes startling in that dark face. And no doubt about it, of royal birth and at least as pedigreed as Pooch herself, or even more so.

"You look ridiculous down there," the Siamese says.

The fat man is still on his knees reaching under the bed from the other side, but now he leans back and sits on his heels. "Well, well, Chloe, may I introduce. . . . This is. . . . Well, who are you?"

Pooch goes to the writing desk and takes a piece of note paper and, having dared so much already, dares again, twice. First she dares to pick up the pornographic crocodile pen, and second, she dares to write *Pucci*, for after all, she once could sing and, evidently, rather well. That is clear from the ad.

"Pucci! And a very charming and accomplished lady, I must say. And now, my dear, if you would like to eat, you must promise me ahead of time that you'll reveal charms and accomplishments of an entirely different sort from those you have already shown me. I am sure you will comply. You would not want the baby to go hungry, would you? And it is obvious that you, also, would enjoy a bit of breakfast."

With that he goes back into the kitchen and returns with two trays of food, each more inviting than the other, with marinated vegetables, green salad, dark bread, two kinds of cheese, and a little bowl of nuts on the larger tray for Pooch.

"I will consider your eating my food as acquiescence to my plans, but now you must excuse me for a moment," he says, putting the trays on the Louis XIV coffee table, "while I go and take my aphrodisiac."

The baby immediately begins to eat and Pooch, of course, cannot bring herself to try to stop it. Since this is the case, she thinks that she might as well eat a mouthful or two herself, though there is no guarantee that, if she eats only a little, she will only have to comply with his sybaritic desires by an amount commensurate with what she has eaten. No, she might as well gobble it all up. Perhaps there is another way out than starving herself.

Chloe now sits opposite them on the floor and, with regal disapproval, watches them eat. It's disconcerting, but even so Pooch doesn't stop the baby from making a mess of it. She does try to counteract that image by eating with all the elegance and grace she can manage, even though this does detract somewhat from her enjoyment.

"Can't you speak?"

Pooch is not absolutely sure, but shakes her head no. She would not want to try again and have barking come out.

"Are you interested in serious questions?"

Pooch gives a little I-don't-know shrug.

"I have heard there are efforts being made. For us, I mean."

Pooch hopes Chloe is not referring to such things as the doctor was doing. She is hoping that, if efforts are being made, they are on an entirely different level than the experiments to which she has been subjected. She makes the I-don't-know shrug again.

"Up or down?"

Pooch points up.

"I also."

Pooch makes a gesture to show that that is obvious. It seems to please Chloe, and her manner softens a bit.

"I'm sorry I scratched your baby," she says.

Pooch gives a forgiving wave of her hand.

"He wears the key around his neck. On a gold chain, no less. A short one. I tried once, but one can't get it over his nose without waking him up."

Just then the fat man returns. He has changed out of his purple silk pajamas and now he wears an embroidered headband and a loose black satin robe with gold braid about the collar. He is carrying three little paper cups with an inch of liquid in the bottom of each one. "I made this outfit myself," he says, "including the embroidery on the headband. I know it doesn't match, but I can't resist wearing it every chance I get, and I wanted you to see the workmanship. Now Pucci. . . ." (In spite of herself, Pooch visualizes it as Poochie.) "Pucci, see to it that the baby drinks this. It's very mild. It'll just make it sleep for an hour or two. It should like it. It's cherry, if you'll pardon the expression. And here are *your* aphrodisiacs. I'll be watching, so don't try to throw them in the dieffenbachia."

Pooch rushes to the writing desk for more paper and the lewd pen. "Kind sir," she writes, "for I know you are kind, I have seen it and felt it." This is not exactly true, but better to err on the side of expecting virtues than the opposite, in the hope of making them come true. "Surely a man of your sensibilities will not ask of me what I have no right to give since it is certainly the property of the man I may one day fall in love with. As the root yearns toward the stalk, as the bud yearns toward its flowering, as the chrysanthemum as well as the delphinium. . . ."

"Enough!" the fat man shouts, reading over her shoulder. "you cannot wriggle out of it. You ate, therefore you promised, and I can see you are not the sort to break your word."

With that he snatches the pen from her and, leaning over her, breathing, deliberately it seems, on the back of her neck, he draws a quick yet practiced rendering of a strawberry. Clearly he is a man well versed in many arts. "But let some others convince you," he says. He opens a book and reads: "'only there, do hearts less etiolated by the thousand little worries of vanity,' vanity it says, my dear, 'find delicious pleasures even in the lesser varieties of love,' lesser varieties, it says. 'For I have seen far more furious transports and moments of intoxication caused by a caprice,' caprice it says! 'than were ever brought about by the wildest passion here in the longitude of Paris.' So. No more stalling. Come, both of you. Take your aphrodisiacs."

Pooch decides there is nothing for it but to do so.

The fat man turns out the lights (anyway, it is now dawn) and, with a little Baryshnikov flourish, leaps onto the bed. "First you two be Tristan and Isolde for a while," he says, "and then I'll be Queen of the Night. I want to save myself for last."

CHAPTER X
In Which the Baby Saves Them Both

> And so, after all, his acquaintance with
> the languages of dogs, frogs, and birds
> was of as much use to him as if he had
> been a man of great learning.
>
> *Grimm's Fairy Tales*

Pooch does not want to sink into licentiousness. Perhaps if she comports herself with the utmost decorum. . . . But already the aphrodisiac is beginning to take effect and Pooch's mind turns, of its own accord, to the pale, thin young man with tan eyes and tan hair who must have been the one singing the part of Escamillo. She feels sure that, were he here, he would be as kind to her as her beloved master used to be. Hadn't she seen that in his eyes? Hadn't she smelled it? Why, even the faint whiff of sexual interest? Perhaps he lives nearby and might rescue her any minute now. She would say yes to him. Yes, yes, yes, and yes, she thinks (remembering Joyce's *Ulysses*). . . . But Pooch knows this is only a silly wish that cannot be.

Several little yelps of passion now escape her in spite of herself. Quite uncouth, really, and then she, along with the other two, falls across the king-sized bed in a semiswoon, her master, the pale young man, the dark, evil (or perhaps only misguided) doctor, and even the psychologist, all swirling together into a single sexy being.

★   ★   ★

Meanwhile, at the little opera house on Third Avenue, they have found the rolled-up blue smock with what looks like blood on it and have turned it over to the police, whom the pale-eyed young man has just reluctantly told of the young thing at the stage door dressed in what he now realizes were bits and pieces from the cast-off costumes of *Cavaleria Rusticana;* and the doctor, with bandage on neck and shoulder and looking quite out of character in sneakers and sweatshirt, is skulking about in an entirely different part of town ordering every creature he sees, from Pekinese to canary, to take him to their leader and to be quick about it. At the New York City Opera they have just lost another top soprano, who has run off with a trumpeter swan; and in government offices as well as in institutions of higher learning, secret meetings are in session this very morning on the topic of motherhood. What, for instance, are the alternatives to it should worse come to worst? A decision has already been made to outlaw from the human race all creatures except primates (and of those, only the ones who have passed a certain level of expertise) in order to preserve, as well as possible, future generations from contamination with inferior and outlandish genes. It's a question of priorities, and for once motherhood and related topics seem to be at the top of the list, though it's true they are hoping to find ways of eliminating it altogether. Already research is being done not only in *in vitro* fertilization but also in the coupling of the germ cells from the male only. The present problem would be solved, then, by simply going around it. In the future one would not need to create any humans (so-called humans, that is, for a great deal of doubt has been cast on the status of women as human beings all through the ages of course, but now in particular) . . . at any rate, one would no longer need to create beings with two X chromosomes at all.

And at this moment the president is preparing a talk for television to be aired that very night on the need for control — control in all its myriad forms. Control of self first, of course, for if men cannot control themselves then who can? Second, control of mothers, wives, sisters, daughters, and assorted pets. If all men become responsible for their unruly kin, the basic problem will be solved. Rebellious and grotesque relatives must be caged one way or another, fenced off in wilderness areas or confined to attics, kept out of sight at the very least. Last, and most important of all, of course, is control of the world in general. Masters must be masterful. Governments must remain adamant. And the president will make it perfectly clear that the first priority is not, after all, the question of motherhood, for that question is being solved this very moment by the best research teams in laboratories all across this great land of ours as well as all across other lesser lands; no, the first priority is the question of control. We need have, he will say, no fear that the researchers will fail, and so we dare risk everything.

★   ★   ★

All this while Pooch, though she could be said to be completely out of control, has managed to get through to early afternoon with her virginity intact, partly with the help of Chloe (a masterful and graceful contortionist) and partly because they are all three exhausted long before any such climax is called for. Pooch does learn a lot, though, that she has not even suspected before. Knowledge that may stand her in good stead later on, though she hopes she will be able to use it with someone for whom she has some real feelings. She had not been aware until now, for instance, of the exquisite sensitivity of the breasts, and especially had not been aware that the nipples of the male are, or so it seems, as sensitive as those of the female; nor had she realized the potential for pleasure of the backs of the knees, not to mention the toes and the bottoms of the feet. She also had not realized the many ways that music, ribbons, belts, pepper, and guacamole could be used.

At last, around one in the afternoon, they all three fall asleep, strewn every which way across the bed, Chloe with her arm around Pooch, the fat man's fat leg across both of them, his head on Chloe's back between her shoulder blades. He is now wearing nothing but a black leather posing cup with a large zipper up the center (zipped, as of now) and several heavy bracelets and, of course, the key around his neck. Chloe is wearing a great deal of jewelry. Pooch is wearing the same fringed scarf and the beads and earrings she came in with, though nothing else. There are bruiselike kiss marks on the bodies of both young females.

Of course they are no sooner sound asleep than the baby begins to cry. Pooch drags herself out from under the other two to go see to it, but the baby, usually so easy to calm or to distract, will not stop crying. Pooch wonders if perhaps the sleeping potion disagreed with it. The fat man groans with rage. Chloe lets out a couple of howls of the sort that only a Siamese can make, which set the baby off all the louder. There is no place to go but the kitchen, but now the baby is yelling so loudly that, even with the door shut, it's too much for the other two. The fat man pulls off his key, hands it to Chloe, and pushes her off the bed with his feet. "Get that bitch and that brat out of here," he tells her.

Chloe is, at once, wide awake, her eyes calculating slits, a slight grin at the corners of her mouth. She gets Pooch and the baby out of the kitchen (also grabbing a half pint of cream, a stick of butter, and a small container of smoked oysters). They dress quickly. Chloe, hiding her jewels under a high-necked white dress, looks as though she has stepped straight out of the pages of *Vogue*. All the while the baby (stiff with rage or stomachache, hard to tell which) is screaming and the fat man has a pillow over his head. Chloe unlocks the front door and then locks it carefully behind them and puts the gold chain with golden key around her neck, dropping it under her dress with the rest of her jewelry.

"Are you interested in universal questions such as the ultimate fate of creatures like ourselves?"

Pooch nods vigorously *yes,* but then motions to the crying baby.

"Come on, then, or we'll be late. I saw a flier about it. Perhaps if I give the baby some butter when we get there. Anyway, one of us will be able to go and maybe we can take turns."

The motion of their walking, the sights along the street, and the fresh air all seem to calm the baby, but only a little. It still cries vigorously, and yet looks out at everything.

★　★　★

Back at the opera house on Third Avenue a meeting is about to take place. Representative females from many parts of the city as well as from New Jersey, Westchester, Long Island, and even a contingent from Baltimore, are gathering. Pooch and Chloe find that there is a place to drop off children, and the baby no sooner sees the other children than it stops crying and begins to shout enthusiastically, "Bop, bop, bop!" Pooch is rather upset to see that, when faced with a choice of snacks including sunflower seeds, sardines, and dog biscuits, the baby chooses the dog biscuits. She is wondering if she is a bad influence on it.

After seeing that the baby is settled and happy and gnawing its biscuit, Chloe and Pooch, not sure that they really should be there, hurry into the theater and sit in the back row at the side.

The stage is quite different from what it was when Pooch crept in and watched from the wings the day before. Now there is a large green banner across the top with *SPCAC* on it. Just as the pound is now in the hands of the men, the SPCA has been taken over by the females and is now known as the Society for the Prevention of Cruelty to All Creatures. (Pooch guesses instantly that that is what it stands for.) Bide-A-Wee, a sister organization, operates a Long Island retreat and rest home for those who have exhausted themselves in the service of their cause, though there is some risk of picking up distemper there if one hasn't had one's shots. Also their animal cemetery is one of the few places where females can be buried without question because these days the regular cemeteries won't allow females unless it can be proved beyond the shadow of a doubt that there were no animal qualities creeping out in them.

"Does the female have a soul?" is discussed from many a pulpit these days. Sermons are preached to an almost-all-male congregation, for the females seem to have lost interest in everything but the quality of the earth under their feet and their own fascinating bodies, or so the men say. Also, according to the men, the females sometimes even look up at the stars with equanimity as though the universe were the most natural thing in the world and as if the stars belonged to them. But this is a dreadful denigration. The females have, if anything, the opposite point of view. They believe that the stars, if they belong to anyone, certainly belong to the men, or to other higher beings.

Chloe and Pooch hunch low in their seats and try to look inconspicuous, but of course many notice them and wonder who the two beautiful young things are, so unlike each other both in dress and manner, one so feline and so *Vogue,* the other so canine and so gypsy, yet here they lean their heads together, dozing in spite of the uncomfortable seats.

Suddenly everyone stands up and begins to clap in all their various ways. If they can't clap, they stamp and they all shout out. Pooch, half asleep, wonders why they seem to be calling out, "Rosemary, Rosemary!" Can they really be saying *Rosemary,* or is this part of her dream? Pooch stands up with the others, still groggy, and is shocked into complete wakefulness. There, coming out on stage, are not one but several Rosemarys, eight of them to be exact . . . eight doctor's wives, one of them more hunched over than the others, and, even so, much larger. This one comes forward to center stage and breathes into the microphone in asthmatic groans audible even above the racket. Slowly she straightens to her full six feet six. Her gray clothes split apart down the middle, and as they fall to her feet she pulls up under her chin and lifts off the Rosemary mask. She is still, somehow, Rosemary. One can tell it's basically the same person. Whoever the others are, one knows that this is the one to whom the original Rosemary face belonged and upon which the others are modeled; but what a Rosemary! This is Rosemary the abominable. The abominable snowman . . . or, rather, snowwoman. Savage, silvery white, and abominable, but abominable in all the best ways: abominable to contemplate, abominable to meet in the mountains as well as on the streets of the city, *wonderfully* abominable and on their side! Now she is naked (that is, she is wearing nothing but her heavy fur) except for a green, tan, and brown camouflage vest full of pockets. All the pockets are, obviously, stuffed. She raises her arms above her head for quiet.

Pooch is barking joyously, for the first time not ashamed of her animal sounds, for in this place, and next to Chloe's caterwaulings, hers seems as appropriate a sound as any other. Besides, they are all sisters. They are in this together and here it clearly doesn't matter what sort of beast you are, or came from, or will one day be. How wonderful, Pooch thinks, to be whatever one really is, even if half dog and even if something of the savage wolf, as has proven to be the case with her.

They quickly quiet down, however, under Rosemary's fierce yet calm gaze, until the only sound is that in-and-out of her growling breath at the microphone. Then from behind her the other seven Rosemarys step forward and remove their masks and Pooch is again shocked. She cannot help giving a little yelp. The main Rosemary notices her and acknowledges her with a little wink and an ambiguous smile that looks quite like the old Rosemary she knew from the beginning when everyone at the doctor's was wondering if she was really on their side or not. Pooch can see that she has been forgiven her outburst just now and that Rosemary knows why she did it.

For there, on the stage, one of the smaller creatures taking off a Rosemary mask has turned out to be none other than Basenji! Alive! And dressed, under her Rosemary grays, *à la Zouave.* Basenji looks strong and fierce and African. She is grinning a wicked grin and seems quite unlike her old shy self. Pooch is overjoyed and thinks that she can now rewrite her poem into an ode to the return of a dear, dear friend — not dead after all, but more alive, it seems, than ever and part of a special Rosemary movement. Or perhaps she should write an entirely new haiku (later on, of course, when she feels calmer and more rested) in which Basenji's sleeve brushes something as she goes by, a chrysanthemum probably, and by that subtle gesture the reader will know that she is alive after all. Not the sleeve perhaps, but the voluminous Zouave trousers and, of course, not chrysanthemum, but daisy or wild iris. Yes, wild iris. But, oh, Pooch thinks, if only I too could wear a Rosemary mask like Basenji does. Could be worthy of the honor of it.

But now Rosemary is speaking and her voice is not at all the soft, somewhat wheezy whispering of the Rosemary in the doctor's basement. Clearly that was her way of disguising what her voice had become. Now it rasps out, half roar, half asthmatic attack and as if she must speak slowly in order to get the consonants out clearly. Before she quite gets started there are isolated cries of "A, C! A, C!" scattered throughout the hall and one or two of "All creatures!" Paws, hooves, wings, and fingers raised, pointing toward the ceiling, though actually, in meaning, pointing to the sky, as in "the sky's the limit."

" 'Wake and listen,' " Rosemary is saying, "Nietzsche said it. 'From the future come winds and secret wing beats; and good tidings are proclaimed to delicate ears. You shall one day be the people.' Yes, let the masks be put aside. May we all soon go about as our real selves and take joy in it, saying, yes, yes, to whatever we are."

Everyone calls out, "Yes to me." Pooch, as loud as any of the others, makes what sound she can that comes closest to yes. I will never again be ashamed of what I am, she thinks, and not only not ashamed of myself, but not of any other creature no matter how small or wretched or ignorant, and no matter if I can only speak in grunts. I will even honor my voice though it is now a bark and a far cry from what it once was. Tears are flowing across her downy cheeks and onto her lips and she licks them up. Isn't this one of the things the psychologist had been telling her all along? And yet she was not ready to hear it. Hadn't he said something about, if you are not you, who will be you? Who, indeed, she wonders, will be Pooch, if not she?

Rosemary is continuing. "They say we are suffering from a dangerous, virulent form of cancer. Is this cancer?" She holds her great glistening arms out on each side and turns around, doing a little dance step, surprisingly graceful for one so large and heavy. She shimmies, making fun of herself, and colors ripple on her iridescent shadow sides.

"Are these cancers?" Rosemary points to the others on the stage and now Basenji and all of them turn around, each doing her own little dance step. Basenji does a dance that looks rather Egyptian. Pooch recognizes it as such from her knowledge of *Aïda*.

"And now you!" Rosemary roars it out, and they all get up and dance around in their various ways, changing places and kissing and hugging each other. Pooch holds, in turn, the coarse haired, the soft haired, dry scales, stiff back feathers, downy front ones, warm bare skin. . . . It feels good.

"Must one call this a disease? And if so isn't it rather some sort of disease of waking up? So I say go ahead, make a noise and let the breasts flop. We'll be there no matter where they look, however far off into the distance it may be. No promontory without one of us, no heath or tundra or oasis.

"And I want to tell you where else they will be seeing us, for, as of yesterday, the circus belongs to *us!* It's no longer Barnum and Bailey's, but Virginia, Jane, and Corinne's. Though I must say that the circus has *always* been good to us as well as to the very small and the very large."

Of course everyone shouts "Hooray" at the good news. Pooch feels encouraged because, if worse should come to worst and her voice never returns to her, perhaps she could get some sort of job there, however humble it might be. She would certainly be happy, though of course not as happy as if she were an opera star, but happy enough even if useful only to bring the elephant lady her buckets of tea.

And now Rosemary has squatted down on her haunches, her big arms hanging in front of her and her voice softer, and everyone settles back again and is quiet.

"What of motherhood? you are asking. Many of you have read of that in the papers. But having the baby, that's the easy part. It's what happens *after* that that they have to solve. Up all night many a night *and* all day, too. One poor parent is hardly enough. So let not, now or ever, one creature stand in the place of two or two kinds.

"What of the fear of success in all of us females? you are asking, but I say it is not a question of success at all. To stand on the mountain top with flags is not our way, nor should it be. Ask yourselves, can the sea do without the shore, or the fire neglect its fuel? Can seeds fly to their sprouting places without the wind? Does smoke rise without air? None exist without partners. It is high time. Yes, high time! And times to come, as high or higher. . . ."

But there are sounds of scuffling and shouts from the lobby. Quickly the seven other "Rosemarys" on stage help the huge white Rosemary back into her gray dress and mask so that when the dozen or so policemen burst through the doors, guns drawn, there is only this frightened, hunched-over little old lady at the front of the stage.

"Quiet! Don't anybody move!"

But no one is moving and there's no need to call for quiet.

"Give us the one called Isabel and we'll leave you to your Ladies Auxiliary." The tallest one is saying it, but he is not as tall, by any means, as Rosemary when she stands up straight. "Which one is she?" He's not asking that question of all of them, but of a pale young man, tan sweater, tan pants, tan hair, tan eyes, standing beside him. It is *the* pale young man of the day before. Pooch sees that he is staring straight at her. She flinches, shudders, but keeps looking back at him, not hangdog. For once not that, for her sisters here, and Rosemary's words, and Basenji, alive, have changed her. And yes, some electricity is passing between them in that look.

Now all the policemen are looking at her.

"Which is she? She's dangerous."

But the young man looks away and they all look away, too.

That utterly static . . . that stopped, magic moment! As though they were alone. What had she seen in his eyes? What he in hers? A recognition? A kind of joy? She feels so glad to see him. Surely he won't. . . . He can't. . . ."

"Gold fringed scarf. Some of the fringe detached." The big policeman is reading from a list. "Fake jade earrings. Plastic beads, torn skirt with broken zipper. . . ." It doesn't sound as nicely dressed as Pooch had, all this time, felt herself to be. But there's no time to dwell on that, she is already on the floor crawling and the others are rustling and moving, forming a sort of undulating audience in order to hide her as she makes her way not to the nearest exit, but toward the room where, a short time ago, she left the baby. And although Pooch doesn't know it, Chloe, also on the floor, her white dress already irreparably smudged, is heading in the opposite direction, and one or two others are crawling around in a similar fashion just to create confusion.

The policemen fire two shots into the ceiling and yell again for silence, which only causes more confusion. Some creatures deliberately become hysterical, though they have no idea how the police will react to them. But the men pay no attention, and separate at a command, a few to each exit. But by then Pooch is in the room with the children. While the men are rushing out and down the streets and alleyways, she rather tearfully (for she still likes them no matter how they were described) trades her scarves, beads, and earrings for paint rags and an old shirt the children had been using as a smock. Also (wonder of wonders), handed to her by the gentle nanny-goat-like creature in charge of the children, a Rosemary mask.

"Don't leave yet," the creature says. "Might as well begin a painting."

Pooch finds that, distracted and frightened as she is, and though not good with colors, she has a bit of artistic talent besides being musical. She paints a portrait, quite a good likeness of her beloved master, though the eyes are definitely the eyes of her psychologist.

CHAPTER XI
The Call of the Wild

Daphne has escaped the god's
embraces, which, promising love
would but result in ungraceful fertility.
T. E. Hulme

Is not virtue, after all is said and done, invariably triumphant?
Or is it?

Pooch wonders whether, first, one wouldn't have to define the
terms. One would probably have to interpret *triumphant* quite
broadly in order to make it *invariably* triumphant. And therefore
wouldn't it often happen, in the end, that the triumph might be
just in the mind of the virtuous as she falls in defeat? But also,
how would one define *virtuous?* And, whatever it is, has she
herself, though always trying hard, really been it? What of the
episode with the sybarite, for instance, and of the fact — yes, it is a
fact — that she . . . well, more or less, wanted to? What of her
vicious attack on the doctor? Though was it not for the baby's
sake? Has she not always remained faithful to the baby and to her
beloved master as well as to his principles? But has she remained
faithful to her sex . . . to her sisters? Lived up to the SPCAC
standards? Has she remained faithful to the earth in the way that
Rosemary was talking about it — the earth as the mother of us all?
Has she had the presence of mind to worship, now and then, the
sun as well as the dirt she walks on? Has she ever hugged a big
tree? Or even a small one for that matter? Has she chewed grass
recently? Perhaps today can be a day for all those things and not
to worry about how she's dressed. Virtue, after all, wears many
faces. She should be proud, even without her earrings and such.

By now the baby seems to have gotten over its first fear of her
in the Rosemary mask and paint rags. Or maybe bouncing along

outside with plenty of things to see has distracted it. Also it has another dog biscuit to chew on. In fact, Pooch herself is chewing on one too, though reluctantly. She read the list of ingredients on the package and they seem to be made mostly of cereals and dried milk, being specially formulated for puppies, but there was also mention of bone meal. *Whose* bones? she wonders. Still, she must keep up her strength if she's to be any good to anybody. Would her comrades at the pound deny her this? In similar circumstances *she* would be only too glad to help a hungry friend as long as the friend had no other source of food and was actively trying to prevent the whole business of pet food from animal sources. Pooch hopes soon to be involved in that struggle as well as in promoting social change in many other areas, if only things would settle down and she could be free for such activities. But right now she is happy enough to have a nice little bag full of the biscuits. She promises herself she will not eat more than just this one because, anyway, they must be saved for the baby. It is certainly not a very fancy supper compared with the night before. Pooch begins to drool in earnest at the thought of the nuts, sprouts, seeds, and salad of that meal that seems to have happened so long ago, but was, in truth, only yesterday.

It's uncomfortable in the mask, and it smells. That, coupled with the linseed oil and turpentine smells of her shirt-smock and skirt of paint rags, make it hard for her to catch the important smells of the city around her. Also, with the mask, she finds it hard to see out of the corners of her eyes, and her own breath makes it sticky and damp in there. Still, she doesn't dare take it off. The police are everywhere. Pooch knows she must get out of the neighborhood as quickly as possible, or at least off the street. She has found a way of walking that looks like an old lady's but also makes good progress away from the opera house. It's a kind of limp-wobble, the left foot taking a long and efficient stride and the right one taking a short kind of hop. The baby loves it.

But where to go?

Suddenly she remembers Valdoviccini, the name and telephone number that she had seen in the *Opera News* and that are engraved forever on her mind. Of course she can't talk on the telephone. What would he think, answering the phone and hearing only whining, or barks and growls? She can't call, but she can look up the address and go there. She finds a not-bad piece of paper in a trash basket and then finds a drugstore with a phone book. Unfortunately the baby suddenly notices her mask and begins to cry—loud, furious cries. It had forgotten that it was with this creature with an entirely different face, different clothes, and a strong smell of paint.

Pooch starts over, looking for another drugstore, this time being careful to hold the baby backward over her hip in such a way that it can't see her face. By making writing motions she manages to borrow a pen from the drugstore man. She finds there are two addresses for Valdoviccini, one on Central Park West, the other right here in the neighborhood, only a few blocks away. She writes them both down at the top of the paper. Then she tears it carefully in two and on the better, neater half she writes, I am she whom you seek.

The drugstore man is very sweet, and when Pooch tries to return the pen he says to keep it, so now she has a yellow push-button pen. She's never had a pen of her own before. It's a bit of a consolation for having lost her nice clothes. (She misses them even though, from the policeman's description of them, they weren't all that great.) She's thinking that, if there's ever time for it, she'll practice a little sketching. Perhaps try to do the baby. She's sure she can find some more paper in the trash. The drugstore man also gives the baby a lollipop and a balloon. Pooch worries about the baby's brand new teeth and also that it might get used to sweets, but maybe just this once. After all, she has allowed herself a dog biscuit.

Walking away, the pen in her pocket, the balloon blown up (it is red and matches the lollipop) and tied to the baby's wrist by a green-and-white string, and the baby with a new word ("boon-boon"), Pooch is optimistic. Surely Valdoviccini, once he knows who she really is, will save her, hide her. He'll let her rest a while and then, of course, her voice will come back (perhaps with the help of a little more psychotherapy), and he'll see to it that she gets the very best coaching. She is thinking of him as a fatherly man rather like the nice man at the drugstore. She could be loyal to someone like that. Come thick or thin. She can hardly wait for the chance to be that.

She feels so good she begins to think of Carmen's *"L'amour est enfant de Bohème,"* as well as *"Oiseau rebelle."* She, also, both gypsy child and rebellious bird. She even tries to hum as she walks along, but only a kind of monotone growling comes out and she quickly thinks better of it. She doesn't want to attract attention to herself as wild creature with indigestion or some such.

But here she is on Stuyvesant Street, with an ever-increasing sense of déjà vu. Even through the mask it smells of last night. Here, the very door and the whiff of her own pee. Oh, the shame of that . . . she, no better than a puppy! She checks the piece of paper again to make absolutely sure of the address. Yes, Valdoviccini — it must be true — is none other than the sybarite! And so there is no hope. Not even if her voice came back would she ever go near that man again. Now there's nothing to aspire to. She crumples up the message she has written and throws it at his door.

Tears flood the inside of her mask. She turns away, utterly blinded by them, and dashes off forgetting her special old lady's wobble. At the next corner she runs straight into the arms of the pale young man. Nearly knocks him down, and herself and the baby, but his arms are around her, steadying her.

"Are you all right?"

She doesn't answer, either with nod or whimper, but holds on to him like the baby is holding on to her.

He helps her over to the bench in front of the Second Avenue Deli. If she could speak she'd tell him she'd be loyal to him until death parted them and that he should never let go of her elbow. She leans close, her head almost on his shoulder, wanting to collapse at last, but then they both notice that the baby is choking on the lollipop and is rapidly turning from red to blue. How thoughtless of her to career off like that without even being able to see where she was going, endangering the poor little thing, and now thinking only of comforting herself in the arms of someone she hardly knows.

For a minute they are both occupied with turning the baby upside down and pounding its back. Thank goodness the lollipop pops out easily. It lands in the dirt under the bench and the baby immediately wants it back, calling it "boon-boon," which balloon is now but a limp piece of rubber.

"Wait here," the young man says, "I'll get your grandchild another one and a new balloon, too."

Grandchild! Pooch has forgotten that she is wearing the Rosemary mask. She had thought to be relating to him as young thing to young thing . . . even musical young thing to musical young thing, but of course it isn't so. She doesn't dare reveal to him who she really is and it's too painful not to. She doesn't wait. With the baby shouting, "no, no," she takes off heading north, remembering this time to limp, to imitate the old woman he takes her to be. She is calm, sad, determined, facing the bitter world.

There is — she's heard about it — a central park. That must be a good place for the females these days. (She first thinks of trying to get herself to Bide-A-Wee for a long rest and then even perhaps a visit to the master, who lives not far from there — in those halcyon days she could even faintly hear and smell the animals — but where to get the money for the ticket on the Long Island Railroad?) Yes, she'll go to the central park and she'll be careful, for the baby's sake, not to run around senselessly in selfish sorrow, even though she hardly cares whether she lives or dies. Grandchild indeed! And he was the one person, of all people, she had hoped would find her attractive.

After hopping along for half an hour, she throws away the yellow pen in a self-destructive gesture. Why should she bother drawing after all? It's singing that she always cared about. Anyway, the pain of not having the pen is more bearable than the other pains. Perhaps she threw it away for that reason. Now she can mourn one nice yellow pen and not think of anything else, especially not of that monster, Valdoviccini, who, by being what he is, has ruined all her hopes for the future.

By the time Pooch reaches the southern tip of the park, it's already almost dark. She enters cautiously. Decides she now dares take off her mask. What a relief to be out of it (even though it was of Rosemary)! And the baby fast asleep. It had finally forgotten about the balloon and lollipop, had chewed several more dog biscuits along the way, and is now tired and satisfied. How good the smells without the mask! How cool the breeze on her face! Perhaps life is not so bad after all. She moves at a dog-trot farther into the park. Now and then she sees the glint of phosphorescent eyes, now and then hears rustlings, whisper-ings. . . . Night birds squawk, small hunched-over creatures scurry away as she passes. Most likely sisters. She feels more or less at home here and is only a little frightened.

After a while she begins to look for a good tree to hug and to be with for the night. She finds one with scrubby bushes under it that will make a good shelter, puts the baby down, does hug the tree, chews on some grass growing nearby and then eats one more dog biscuit. She can see the full moon coming up, myste-rious, behind her tree. The world looks so beautiful! She won-ders how one can not do for it anything that needs to be done, or at least all one *can* do. She lies down with her cheek pressed against the dirt. Better, she thinks, and more fragrant than any other pillow, even one made of the down from the belly of one of her sister creatures—Mary Ann, for instance. (Not to belittle *them*, of course, for down is nice also and has its own wonderful qualities and had she a down pillow she would certainly be glad of that, too.) She resolves that, from now on, she will try not to be led astray by her old, useless ambitions to be an opera star. Except, is she not a little like Micaela right now and is not this night like the moonlit night of the smugglers and the gypsies? It's a comforting thought. Like living in an opera even if one can't be singing in one. With that she falls asleep.

★ ★ ★

It is the howling that wakes her. Tired as she is, having slept so little the night before, she is now instantly wide awake and the hairs rise on the back of her neck. In spite of herself, and without a single thought for the sleeping baby, she creeps out from under the bushes on all fours. It sounds as if the howls are not far away. Where are they? Where *are* they? She leans back, raises her head, and finds herself letting go with a similar yowl. And they answer. She calls again and they answer again. Then she slinks off toward their sound (still on all fours), and there they are, three large males and an assortment of bitches, one bitch still wearing the remnants of a green silk blouse and with a fine gold chain around her neck, yet almost all wolf now. Some of the other females have no sign that they were ever other than what they are right now. Some have patchy fur, though perhaps that's just mange. A few others have overly long hair on their heads and one is still mostly bleached blonde. One wears a pair of broken glasses. The largest male, heavy and handsome, light tan belly with black back and black markings on his face (black over the eyes and black line down the nose and pricked up wolf ears edged in black, certainly a distinguished specimen of the dominant sex). . . . He's the one who comes up to her first and smells her all over. She stands still. He likes what he smells. She can tell. The others are more suspicious, but they will accept her because he does. Now they move away from the trees and out into the "sheep meadow" to get a better view of the moon. She goes with them. Oh, mooooon! Ah, mooooon! What wonders, not only in the universe, but right here, the view from this planet! Oh, the infinity of time! Ah, the infinity of space! She's seen all that on TV and understood it and understands it even better right now. Yes, and is not this that she's doing right now also singing?

The biggest male is watching her. He, too, loves her voice. Now he licks her face and puts a paw on her shoulder. Now he looks deep into her eyes. How comforting it is to be licked all over and wanted and noticed and how nice to be listened to and to be proud of her voice.

He walks back and forth in front of her, displaying his massive shoulders, broad head, powerful neck. She could, it is clear, become the head bitch of the pack with him as her protector. And what a nice smile he has. But the wolf-bitch is jealous. She was his before Pooch came. Pooch can smell that and see it, too, for the wolf-bitch has, all this time, not howled, but is sitting despondently several yards from the others. Pooch is coming to her senses in spite of the moon. She is realizing that, handsome and alluring as he is and even with that nice smile and gentle touch, the big male is not for her, but belongs to someone else and is probably fickle besides. The psychologist might have told her that she should think of her own pleasure, but she isn't sure what he would say if that pleasure involved a male creature who so clearly belonged to someone else. The wolf-bitch looks so sad, and Pooch has never wanted to cause pain to a sister. Aren't they all females in this together? And yes, this would certainly be a *liaison dangereuse* in more ways than one.

Pooch goes over to the wolf-bitch to apologize, to tell her, in gestures, that everything will be all right for her and that she should come back and howl away with all of them, but the creature turns on her ferociously, tearing her smock and then grabbing her ear. It's very painful. And then, suddenly, they are all after Pooch. Except for the big male, that is. In fact it is he who helps her break free from them. She runs back to her tree, gathers the baby up, though leaving her bundle with the dog biscuits. She has one advantage over them. By now she can climb, even though she's never tried it before, and her tree has nice lower crotches that she can pull herself up into. Of course she won't go very high, this being her first climb ever, but no great height is needed. She stops just out of reach, now hugging the tree in earnest. The dogs leap up, but can't get at her. Then they find the remaining biscuits, gobble them up, little caring what or who they are made of, and troop off with a few lingering howls and snarls. She listens to them moving farther and farther away, and feels a pang of regret for what cannot be. The baby, too frightened to cry while the dogs were snarling underneath, now begins to whimper and Pooch turns to comfort it.

She has shocked herself. Even her pangs of regret, shocking! There seem always to be more depths to which she can sink. To have been almost . . . well, actually to have been infatuated with a large dog! How could she have allowed herself to fall to that level when it is so much fun, and hard work too, being and becoming a human being! Howling at the moon is all well and good in its place, and who's to say that her emotions during that time were not enhanced by her knowledge of exactly what she was howling at? Hasn't she, now, much more to howl about? Much more to make her dizzy and worshipful when she looks up? But she wonders what would have happened had she not felt pity for the wolf-bitch. Thank goodness for that. Virtue can, after all, bring some kinds of victories. A sure sign that she must continue to be as virtuous as possible. *Liaison dangereuse,* indeed! Partly it was those very words that saved her. Could *he* ever have understood them? Not that there is anything wrong with a handsome animal going on being a handsome animal and doing the best he's capable of. And she had certainly appreciated his gentleness and his interest in her. She might have had quite a good life with him for a while, but what of the baby then? And what of all her efforts to better herself? Is this the one she wants as the father of her children? Yet how lonely she is! To be part of a group such as they are would not be all bad. And to raise her voice again, whether in real song or not, how wonderful *that* was. But why not? She tips her head back and howls: Moooooowwn! Oh wonderful moooooowwwwwyyyn!

And Valdoviccini, from his Central Park West apartment (utterly different from his East Village *pied à terre*) hears her and feels the hairs rise on the back of his neck just as Pooch's had but half an hour ago. He opens the window. Thinks that that is by no means an ordinary voice. What mysterious, musical creature is abroad this moonlit night? He, like everyone in the neighborhood, is used to strange sounds coming from the park, but men are more careful about going there than they were, even back in the days when they were afraid only of other men. Valdoviccini is torn. He might almost dare to enter the park in search of that magical voice. Could it be the same voice he has been searching for these past few weeks? The voice that he has yearned to hear again, no matter if still raw and untrained? Is there not in it that same wild sense of "grain" that Barthes was so fond of? And didn't he catch, afterward, the faint cries of a baby? Perhaps the very baby she had had back at the New York City Opera? And then what about the cryptic message he had found crumpled up near his doorway downtown? "I am she whom you seek." What of that?

But no. He shuts the window. Going out into the park on a night such as this would be sheer folly.

CHAPTER XII
A Disturbing Phone Call

> My spirit no longer wants to walk on
> worn soles.
>
> *Friedrich Nietzsche*

As soon as Pooch became aware that the baby's cries had begun to sound like her own howls at the moon, she stopped instantly. How dreadful that the poor little thing has no one to imitate but herself; and who knows to what depths she might sink and already has.

Now she ties the sleeping baby to the branch and herself also, with bits of her paint-rag skirt, and settles down to rest as best she can, back against the tree trunk. She can't get out of her mind what she almost did, and she wonders if she is now descending the evolutionary scale rather than ascending. She begins to examine herself in the moonlight to see if she can tell. First her hands. How graceful they are and what wonderful things to have, these manipulating hands as graceful as wings! Perhaps even more so. She peers at them closely, wondering if hers are turning back into paws. They still have a slightly dappled look, particularly the left. Even in the moonlight Pooch can see that, but can't tell if it is less or more.

Now she strokes her face. (How sensitive those wonderful fingertips!) She finds there are still three or four stiff whiskers on her cheeks but one falls off as she touches it, and she thinks that's a good sign. Back where her cheeks meet her neck she feels a slight fringe of deeper down than on her face and then a little more at the back of her neck, but is it less or more than before? She feels her hips, nicely rounded. Much more so, it seems to her, than before. She pulls up her shirt and sees her several lower nipples almost faded out altogether and the top two larger and nicely rounded. She looks lower. Pubic hair clearly three colors, the white and then the darker spots that she knows in daylight would be black flecks and tan. Nice long legs. Shapely. Pale in the moonlight. Nothing dappled there, but then there never had been.

Ah, but is it not the mind that is the real grace of Homo sapiens? All the things to think about! All the things to read and appreciate! All the arts! All the things of the spirit! Well, no, she did have things of the spirit even before. She was as kind and loyal and honest as she could ever be, she's sure of that. But now she can express it in art. Maybe if she could compose a haiku right now, it would be proof that she's still as human as ever or, as she hopes, even more so. Of course to be Homo sapiens — knowledgeable man — is beyond her still, but it's certainly something to aim for, though she will need a lot more study and work to achieve that status. But the haiku. She will compose something about being humble and yet with hands, though how can one really be humble and have hands? After much thought, she finally comes to:

With thumb and forefinger
I pluck an anemone! Oh,
I pick up a small stone!

Is that several syllables too many? If so, change anemone to daffodil or even to rose. But she's too tired to count it again. Working on the poem has soothed her. She falls asleep yearning for somebody to call, my darling. Almost anybody will do. She actually says those words in her sleep twice, even though she hasn't spoken at all for several days. She is dreaming of sexy big black dogs with devilish markings on their faces but with kindly eyes. Thank goodness she forgets the dreams in the morning.

★ ★ ★

Meanwhile the doctor has come back to his house, picked up his mail, and found that one of the prizes he had hoped to win has gone to someone else before he could gather himself together to submit something. This is the coveted Motherhood prize and it involves a good deal of money even for second and third prize which, needless to say, the doctor also didn't win. The irony is that first prize went to a contraption not unlike the doctor's own shock cage. It's called the Responsive Early-Life Playpen and includes the cupcakes and chit dispenser, though not the shock plates on the floor. The prize winner has even included a recipe for carrot-nut cupcakes that contain all the important vitamins and minerals plus bran and protein so that the child need eat little else. Also the cage has two big, kindly, watchful eyes painted in the top right-hand corner. This is a real brainstorm, considering the recent discoveries on the importance of eye contact even to tiny newborn babies. This playpen can be adjusted for ages zero through three by simply inserting different electronic disks and different foodstuffs. Later on one can add a knob on the *inside* of the doorway plus a Jolly-Jump-Up that laughs at jokes and that will lead, by subtle reinforcement, to ever higher forms of humor, all the way up to irony. The pen also comes with a Mother's-Arms device from which to get lots of hugging. This is considered so important that it is stipulated that this addition not be optional, but that all pens must come equipped with it. The government considers the pen unacceptable without it.

The doctor could have adapted his own device to a mothering function. He might even have done a better job than the winner, for he'd have added both physical and mental exercises: a trapeze, toys that teach volume and weight, and problems in (at the very least) Aristotelian logic, with little blocks shaped like > and < and ∴ , etc., so that the child could form its own little syllogisms. The importance of having a child of his own has only just now occurred to him. If only he and Rosemary could have had one. Perhaps it's not too late to adopt. That baby 107 had was really quite interesting, though unpredictable. Why had he not studied it more minutely while he had it at hand?

★ ★ ★

Just after this blow, the doctor receives a disturbing phone call from the police asking him if he is aware that his wife had been seen that very afternoon standing on stage at some sort of feminist meeting, albeit looking frightened and humble. On the whole, the police tell him, it was quite a subversive, rowdy crowd, and he might be interested in looking into it.

He goes to the kitchen to check up on what Rosemary is doing now and sees her just finishing up the dishes, but he catches a glimpse — or thinks he does — of another, smaller Rosemary ducking up the back stairs, and suddenly he remembers that on the way into the house he had seen a third Rosemary down on her knees in the garden. That Rosemary, hardly fifteen minutes ago, had been wearing an old green smock and baggy green work slacks, whereas the other two Rosemarys were wearing black housedresses with tiny yellow roses. He decides to go up and take a little nap. He's had such a hard two days — perhaps he's lost too much sleep.

But on the way upstairs he gets a glimpse out the hall window of yet another Rosemary. This fourth one is quite tatterdemalion and is limping up the front steps with a baby in her arms. Can it be *the* baby? The very one he wants?

He realizes now that there's nothing wrong with *him*, though something very wrong is going on right here in his own house.

There is a coat closet by the front door and the doctor squeezes himself in with the galoshes and coats and leaves the door open about an inch, holding it so it won't close or open any farther. Now he can see out both sides: quite a bit toward the stairway and a little bit, through the hinged side of the door, toward the front vestibule. The bedraggled Rosemary — he had never seen her in such a state as this, so dirty and torn — opens the front door slowly and cautiously and peers inside. Just then the baby gives a big hiccup. The Rosemary jumps back out and shuts the door. There's a long wait. The doctor had just about decided to come out of his hiding place and run outside to see where she had got to when the door swings open again and the Rosemary creeps in, looking first into the living room on the left and then up the stairs. It's clear that this Rosemary has never been here before, or certainly not in this part of the house. The Rosemary hesitates, goes a few steps beyond the stairs, and then turns around and starts up them.

When she turns at the landing, the doctor comes out of his hiding place and slowly creeps up after her. From the landing he can see her scratched and dirty sandaled feet, very un-Rosemarylike. He watches them as she goes from room to room peeking in. Before she gets to the attic door, it opens and the doctor can see two other Rosemary feet in Rosemary brown oxfords come down the steps. The first Rosemary's sandals had retreated in haste, but now they come forward to meet the oxfords. There are whispered exclamations, then a little shriek of delight and another hiccup from the baby and then another. The hiccups don't stop. Quickly the brown oxfords follow the sandals up the steep attic stairs. By the time the doctor reaches the door, it is locked.

There never used to be a lock on this door. Also it feels more solid than it ever was before, as though heavy wood or even metal had been added to reinforce the other side. The doctor pushes as hard as he can, but nothing to be done about it without tools and/or a noisy running start. This is probably not the right time for that. There's a good deal of thinking he must do before taking any irrevocable steps or blowing their cover. For instance, which is the real Rosemary—or *is* there a real Rosemary anymore? Have they done away with her, or are they keeping her prisoner so as to infiltrate his home, no doubt to find out more about his experiments and to study his data and methods to use for their own purposes. Perhaps they tortured his Rosemary into letting them use the attic. Well, the best plan may be to wait until all those Rosemarys that are still out around the house get back in the attic and then he will barricade the door and trap them all up there.

★   ★   ★

It is clear that Pooch has decided to put on her Rosemary mask, straighten herself up as best she can, and return to the only place she knows to find help and where, she's quite sure, all the other Rosemarys must have come from. At least she knows *one* Rosemary is there. Also she does not like thinking of herself as a killer however it might have been justified to save the baby, and she wants to return to the scene of the crime to see if the doctor is really dead or just wounded and if there's anything she can do to help. She feels that, at the very least, she must apologize and somehow find a way to tell Rosemary that she never meant to cause her any pain.

CHAPTER XIII
Trapped

> Never had my eyes beheld anything so
> dappled and motley.
>
> *Friedrich Nietzsche*

What had caused that little shriek of delight the doctor had heard from the bottom of the stairs? It was the fact that the Rosemary (brown oxfords) coming to greet the Rosemary (worn dirty sandals) had been none other than Chloe. It was Chloe who had opened the attic door and realized from many clues who it must be behind the other Rosemary mask. She knew those sandals, too. Actually, from their experience of the night before last, she also knew quite well the knees and elbows and even other parts of the body that she could not see. She had tipped up the corner of her own mask far enough for Pooch to recognize her and it was then that Pooch had given the little shriek and the baby had gotten the hiccups. Chloe had hurried them both up the attic stairway, carefully locking the door behind her with the two huge bolts, one on the doorknob side and the other on the hinge side.

Once upstairs, Pooch and Chloe hug each other so vigorously that the baby begins to cry. But it is soon quieted, for Chloe brings granola bars and milk, and for Pooch a cup of Earl Grey tea from the hot plate. The baby begins to eat right away, but Pooch first hugs Basenji and makes a gesture in admiration of her presence and dancing at the meeting when she was a guard to the "real" Rosemary. Pooch does this with a pretty little bow and silent clapping. And there's Mary Ann to greet. (Later Pooch will find out that she came to be in the attic instead of the basement because the doctor could no longer put up with her looks and her inanities and simply threw her out as not only useless to his work, but a hindrance to it. Of course one of the Rosemarys went after her before she got lost and brought her back.) She is now completely palmiped, though one still cannot tell for sure whether her feathers are those of a swan or of a domestic duck. There are others, whom she doesn't know, one quite green and with big teeth and mouth, and there's even a man — a strange, sad-looking, very thin and very tall man, introduced to her as John, a clown, though dressed now in a conservative brown suit.

The attic room is large and cluttered. In the corner opposite the hot plate is a pile of rolled-up pallets, quilts, and pillows. Undoubtedly, Pooch thinks, what the Rosemarys sleep on. In the center, four antique trunks serve as a table, surrounded by folding chairs, stools, and old porch furniture. It is here that Pooch sits to sip her tea and milk, noticing as she does so the pictures tacked on the walls. There is a great clutter of them, some partly overlapping others and many slanting up into the eaves. All but one are of famous animals. Pooch recognizes many of them without having to look at the captions: Rosinante, Bucephalus, Flush, Checkers, Anubis (just as handsome and sexy looking as the big black-and-tan dog in the park; the picture makes her feel a prickle of awe and excitement), Sirius (also impressive, though Pooch feels no attraction to him — he's not her type), Washoe, Grendel (with his mother), a sacred cow, the god Ganesha, Pavlov's dog (pictured wired up and reminding Pooch of the experiences in the basement), Kashtanka (aka Auntie), Laica . . . . Ah, Laica! Pooch had thought of her often since first reading her story, and it always made her sad. She remembers a poem by Sec about her that ends "Man had never better friend." She hopes also to be a friend to man — perhaps one particular man — in some similar way. But then there is Kashtanka, too. There is certainly a lesson in the fate of that poor mutt, but of course such a fate is not for her, for her master loves her so that she feels more a daughter to him than to her own mother, whom she can barely remember. Looking at them all, Pooch wonders if she might not one day have her own picture among such as these, dressed as Carmen, in red with a black mantilla; though without a voice — not even for speaking — that seems unlikely. Still, if not one way, maybe another. She must not despair.

The one picture that is not of a well-known animal is a large color photograph of five clowns. Two are dwarfs, while one is very tall and very thin, and though he has a large, painted-on smile, Pooch is quite sure it is the same man as the one she has just met wearing the conservative brown suit.

All the while that Pooch is sipping tea and examining the pictures, Chloe is explaining how she came to be there and how she became yet another Rosemary in a little candlelight ceremony at which she had made a solemn promise to uphold Rosemary standards and to work hard to make the world safer for females of whatever shape and size and in whatever state of change, regardless of whether heading upward or downward on the evolutionary scale. She had doubled back, she says, to the SPCAC meeting after helping to create a diversion so that Pooch could escape. The police had been searching everyone as they came out — or rather, trying to, but there was much too much confusion. Some of the creatures, though they can't actually fly, can almost fly, and these had fluttered about, and taken great leaps into the air with the help of their wings, or had sat, poised and unafraid, at the top of the ornamental lintel. Others crept about on all fours and then ran out between the policemen's legs.

Chloe does not mention that she herself had gotten quite carried away and, not being able to hold herself back, had had a great deal to do with all this fluttering about. (Were she at all canine, she surely would look rather sheepish telling about it.) She had chased hither and yon and pounced and had quite a romp, though no real harm done to anyone except for the loss of a few feathers and the tip of one tail, not counting that Chloe herself had gotten a feather stuck in her throat for a while. Very unpleasant. At any rate, the police were thoroughly confused and Chloe had had fun until a creature not unlike herself, but much larger, began chasing *her*. She does not tell this part, but rumbles out her tale, smiling, half in a whisper, half self-satisfied purr. And actually she has already forgotten the episode of being chased up into a tree that was already filled with creatures she had but a moment before chased up there herself.

"Then," she says, "one of the Rosemarys brought me here and we had the ceremony, and after that a very good mackerel dinner to which I contributed my cream, butter, and smoked oysters from Valdoviccini's."

While talking, Chloe has handed the baby to a rather shapeless, fat-cheeked yet sharp-nosed creature with mixed white and orange hair swept back from her face. It is not long before she and Pooch recognize each other, for she is none other than Cucumber (Pickle for short), the very guinea pig who lived down the block back on Long Island. She is much changed, however, being now almost completely a young woman, though a bit dumpy and dull-eyed. Pooch remembers that reflex she used to have: the almost overpowering desire to chase, catch, grab Cucumber by the back of the neck, and shake. Now, thank goodness, that desire seems gone, either because Cucumber is much more a woman or because Pooch is. Or perhaps she's just too tired and grateful to Cucumber for relieving her of the baby for a moment. Pooch hopes that it is the womanliness, the humanity, that has changed her. That would be a good sign, indeed.

They kiss and a tear comes to Pooch's eye, for seeing her brings back memories of happier days with the master and mistress and of the scratchy mat by the door. Difficult as the work had been, she had had several chances to listen to the Saturday afternoon opera and once in a while she had seen Kenneth Clark's "Civilization." A few times she had actually seen these through without interruption. Suddenly Pooch begins to cry in earnest. Actually, though tears have come before, many times and copiously, this is the first real "relaxed" crying she has done since all this began. Though this is not really "home" and her dear master is not here, she is safe and among friends and perhaps even about to be a part of some splendid and noble Rosemary movement.

They all gather round to hug her and stroke her and rub her under the chin, even the tall, thin, sad clown. Chloe heats up her milk, and Mary Ann — flop, flop, flopping about on her wide feet and sometimes tripping over herself—brings out one of the pallets. The green creature with the big teeth sheds a few tears of her own, grinning at the same time, but that's just her way and no harm meant. They put Pooch to bed in a corner, where she falls asleep instantly. While she sleeps, the various Rosemarys return one by one until they are all back except for the one real Rosemary, who is no doubt off on some mission more important than any of the others. Perhaps she has gone to check up on the recently formed Academy of Motherhood.

*   *   *

The doctor does not know how many Rosemarys there are. He waits and counts nine altogether, including the first two (Chloe and Pooch). Then there is a long, long period when none of them come at all. It's growing late. Almost ten o'clock and the doctor has had no supper, or lunch for that matter. He decides that now is the time to barricade the door. He'll do this first, hungry and tired as he is. Of course they will hear him hammering them in, but that won't make any difference. The roof is four stories high and there are no places to perch by the steeply pitched eaves and no places to climb down, even for one as adept as Phillip.

After nailing them in, using spikes and heavy boards, he goes down to make himself some supper, but he's no cook, and anyway he's too tired to do more than eat a few cupcakes from the cage dispenser. Finds they are delicious. He is thinking, thank goodness Rosemary had seen to it that they are full of nourishment. If not for her, where would the experimental animals be? Starved, maybe. He must admit that Rosemary is, has always been, a great help. But what about that phone call from the police? What has she been up to? As far as he can tell, she's always been on his side. But he'll not even call the police about those boarded up in the attic. He decides to get a good night's sleep and then he'll decide what to do about all this. He forgets that there's been no one around, now, what with his locking in all the Rosemarys, to feed his experimental creatures in the basement, or to lock them back into their cages for the night. He even forgets that the window in his laboratory is still unbarred and wide open, arranged as it was for the escape of number 107 with a stool and a bookcase forming a ladder.

CHAPTER XIV
A Festive Dinner Party

> Worms awaken into birds, and music
> bursts from their astonished throats.
> *Tom Disch*

The new Academy of Motherhood and related concerns occupies a building on Fifty-seventh Street. It looks rather like a fortress; indeed, it *is* a fortress, for no one wants motherhood defenseless in the modern world, or at the mercy of primitive forces. Major stumbling blocks are the mothers themselves. (Perhaps in the future a small monetary reward for mothering might not be out of line.) It is hoped that, under the aegis of the Academy of Sciences, motherhood will be modernized and mechanized and become a true science. Certainly it can be at least as scientific as psychology or linguistics could ever be. It is also to be hoped that the Academy of Motherhood will become the place to birth future administrators.

On the ground floor of the motherhood building there is a shop with updated motherhood items. In one section: straps, harnesses, leashes, pens, gates for doorways, tranquilizers, etc. In another section: intercoms, closed-circuit TV, word processors, etc. In another: flow charts, comparison charts of how other children do at the equivalent ages, record-keeping books . . . all the software of motherhood.

So far, the experimental mothers have been kept on the top floors. They are examined every week to see how their unborn babies are coming along and to try to ascertain just what sorts of babies can be expected from any given mother in the throes of any given changes. Former mothers cook and clean for them. The Academy realizes that, no matter how civilized a country may become, there will always need to be people one can leave the dirty work to (as well as the sitting around listening to the nonsense of young people); and who better to leave this work to than mothers and former mothers?

At this very moment a search is under way to find the Maximum Mother (the MM, as she is referred to), so that she may be honored by the Academy. She should have the quiet dignity befitting a mother and yet so rare in mothers. It is hoped that she will exemplify all the best qualities of motherhood and that she will show other mothers that they too can set new records in the field. (It has been so little studied that surely new records will not be hard to set once the mothers are pushed in the direction of efficiency and dignity.)

The Academy of Motherhood, with its thick walls and small windows that don't open, will surely be one of the last, if not *the* last, buildings to fall into the hands of the opposing forces should it ever come down to that. That is as it should be: motherhood as the last bastion of the reliable, the reasonable, the sane, and the scientific.

The Academy is surely the best place for the doctor to call in the morning after his good night's sleep. It would, he is thinking, serve all those Rosemarys right if they were forced to become experimental mothers. Yet he hopes his own Rosemary is safe. He wonders if perhaps he still loves her. But why not? She's never given him cause not to. He hopes she's not been kidnapped and brainwashed.

But now the doctor is dreaming of a huge, engulfing Rosemary rolling over him . . . a kind of wave, and he is tumbled about in her surf, helpless. It's scary, but it's also exciting, sexy. Nonetheless, he wakes up screaming. It's three in the morning. And now the door to his bedroom is opening slowly and a Rosemary is coming in. (It's been a long time since they slept in the same room, and it's been a long time since she dared to open the door and walk in like this without even knocking; though, of course, it's also been a long time since he shouted out in his sleep.) He is instantly wide awake and poised. Ready. She comes closer, leans over him so that he can smell the rubber mask and hear her asthmatic wheeze. In the dim light from the hall he can see her familiar lumpy silhouette, though since he's lying down he can't get any sense of her size. What sort of Rosemary is this? he wonders. Thinks it most likely can't be "his" Rosemary since she's wearing a mask. He waits for her to lean even closer, then grabs the mask and rips it off, and, in the next gesture, turns on the bedside light, pieces of torn rubber dangling in his hand.

She looms, swells up, glitters. Yes, it *is* she. "His" Rosemary. Got to be. The one he used to love. Might love even yet and in spite of everything. My God! Staring at him. The Great Mother. What he wants to do is bow down. What he wants to talk about is love. Wants to bask in her shadow. Lie at her feet. Say, "I've always loved you," and all of a sudden, he thinks he has.

"I want you to call the Motherhood Academy first thing in the morning," she says. "I want you to turn us all in to them. Myself included."

It's clear to the doctor that, for all her changes, and in spite of all the Rosemarys in the attic, "his" Rosemary has been on the side of reason all along. (Should he suggest that she put herself up for the Maximum Mother award?) "I will, I will," he says, so eager to please that he jumps out of bed. But now he can see how big she really is (compared to his six feet three), and the light is just right for her to be at maximum shimmer. Awed, he says aloud what he thought a moment ago: "I've always loved you." He is remembering a quote from Marcus Aurelius: "Does the emerald lose its beauty for lack of admiration? Does gold, or ivory, or the color purple?" But right after that he remembers that Marcus Aurelius also said: "Never allow yourself to be swept off your feet: when an impulse stirs, see first that it will meet the claims of justice." He will be cautious. This may be a trap to get on his good side. Or a way to infiltrate the Academy of Motherhood and take over powers of motherhood for themselves. Is it too late to take back the assertion of love?

Rosemary doesn't bother answering his words of love. She probably knows him better than he knows himself, or perhaps she's lost interest in whatever he may think of her. "As to the creatures in the basement," she says, "you will find they have already fled through the laboratory window. The poor things are, however, without suitable clothes and will not get far, especially of they stick together, which I presume they will. They'll have 'inmates' written all over them. I expect they'll be returned soon. Come. Let's make a meal for them. They have not even had any supper, poor babies."

As a matter of fact, the phone does ring just then and the doctor is informed that his experimental animals have been rounded up and will, in a few minutes, be delivered to his door. At first they had been mistaken for a group of prostitutes in the wrong part of town, which is why they had been arrested, and then it was decided to take them to the pound. But when they heard this the creatures, with Phillip as their spokesman, had confessed that they were part of the doctor's important experiments and wished to be returned to him.

Together the doctor and Rosemary go down to the kitchen, where he intends to keep an eye on his wife. Actually, he can't keep his eyes off her. How fast and efficiently she moves about, mixing, pouring, turning things on and off almost in the same motion! She is puffing and wheezing, but that does not detract in the slightest from her glamour. In fact it somehow makes her even larger than the larger-than-life she already is to him. There hardly seems room for them both in the spacious kitchen, and every time her fur touches him as she passes it gives him prickles up and down his spine. He has a hard time keeping Marcus Aurelius in mind. He wonders if he should read Ovid instead.

"One of these days—I hope soon—I will join my fellow hyperborians," Rosemary says. "My body is not designed for these latitudes." She is at this moment chewing on an ice cube. The doctor wonders if she is warning him of the impossibility of their ever having a life together in the future.

Rosemary ties an apron around the doctor's waist and sets to cooking the kibble and sunflower-seed pancakes while she gets out carrots, celery, tea, and cream, along with mealworms and chocolate-covered ants. Clearly the meal is to be a special treat.

In spite of trying hard not to enjoy himself, the doctor has not had so much fun in a long time. He remembers when, at around the age of eleven, he could flip pancakes by throwing them up with the pan. In a moment of youthful exuberance he tries this, though not successfully. Rosemary neither scolds nor laughs, but wipes up the mess, as deadpan as ever. You'd almost think her big white-with-black-markings face was another mask and that all her silvery glitter was another costume under which was yet one more Rosemary, and then below that another, each one miraculously larger than the one before and each face even less expressive.

She has set the table in the main dining room with the Rosenthal china and the Gorham flatware, and when the police deliver the basement inmates they are invited into the front dining room instead of being ushered down to their cages. It is the doctor, still in his pajamas and slippers and wearing the large, flowered apron, who serves them and sees to it that their plates and cups are never empty.

In this setting the natural elegance of all the creatures becomes clear. Phillip's especially. One cannot deny that her colors are a bit on the garish side to be considered truly refined, but one cannot help appreciating her sinewy grace, her proud head and smile (though perhaps that constant little upward curl to the lips should not be called a smile at all). It is she who, automatically, sits at the head of the table and keeps an eye out to see that everyone is eating. It is clear that she is the one who masterminded the escape effort and that she will take advantage of any other opportunity that may come her way, though now that Rosemary—and a completely new Rosemary, at that—seems to be in charge even of the doctor, Phillip is obviously confused.

The doctor wonders if he should warn Rosemary about Phillip. Yet he hesitates to do so. He can see the same alert, wary look on the faces of both of them, and he wonders if they are in this together, even though it is apparent that Phillip, like the others, has never seen this particular Rosemary before, or rather, this particular aspect of her. It is also clear that they are all, Phillip included, both shocked and pleased to have found such a powerful ally. But that was exactly how the doctor himself had felt on first seeing her. He knows he should be doubly wary, since it seems that all creatures who come under Rosemary's spell feel that they are home at last. (A good characteristic for the Maximum Mother. The doctor is wondering again if he should urge her to try out for it, though he knows this is motherhood at its most dangerous.)

As they eat they do not speak. Perhaps they are inhibited by the presence of the doctor and by this strange, imposing Rosemary, and of course by the elegant setting—the almost see-through tea cups, the water in cut-glass wine glasses—but all their natural animal refinement comes to the fore and the doctor is not at all bothered by a nervous flutter or flap or any inadvertent squeaks. He is as pleased with them as though he had trained them himself for just this occasion and now finds them using the right fork at the right time, which they do. Even tired as they are, only one cup of tea is spilled and only a few mealworms slither away.

Almost without forethought, at the end of the meal the doctor brings out brandy snifters and his VSOP and proposes a toast. It's Rosemary he toasts, as seems only fitting—also expedient under the circumstances—but it is to Phillip that he raises his glass and his eyes. Rosemary has gone beyond him and, though splendid, is in fact on the way down and one must not forget it, while Phillip. . . . But of all of them in the basement, Phillip has never been impressed by *him*. On the contrary (and that may be one of her appeals). She has never been girlishly giddy, nor has she ever lost sight, as far as he could tell, of just exactly what the situation in the basement was. Also he must admit he has not treated her very well, though of course that was for the sake of scientific enquiry. He hopes she understands that. And that time when she said what a privilege it was and what a joy to be becoming human. He had not listened. He had not believed. And here she is, fierce joy apparent in every motion, and looking more human and more gorgeous than ever even though her blue smock does not bring out her natural coloring at all. In fact clashes with it. Here she is, modeling proper fork use to the others, though she does it almost as a putdown of proper manners—almost as a challenge. She's a combination the doctor cannot resist. It promises so much in the way of both knowledge and surprises.

Perhaps even joy, and it's been a long time since the doctor thought about anything even remotely connected with joy.

Shortly after the toast they all go off to their cages to sleep for the few hours that remain of the night. All but the doctor, that is. Try as he will, he cannot go back to sleep. He is wondering, where does the truth lie, with motherhood and the Academy? Or with these forces of the animal? He wonders if there is any hope for him to have a future with Phillip *without* changing his allegiances . . . have a future with *any* female? Yet doesn't he owe his very existence to motherhood? Shouldn't he therefore remain loyal to the Academy? But where does Rosemary stand in all this? Hard to tell. And which side will win in the long run? Not that that should influence his choice. Should he try to stop them now, though they are doing exactly what he would have told them to do if they had asked his advice? How logical Rosemary is! Most of them are all id. Phillip especially. No, that's not true. She's both. Is that best? Has he been misled by logic? Is it logical to be so logical? Perhaps he should go with his feelings. For Phillip. Now *she's* one who knows how to use the butter knife for the butter and a fork for the mealworms.

In the morning the doctor will try to convince Rosemary that Phillip should be left behind with him and not turned in to the Academy of Motherhood with the others. He can't bear the thought of her being inseminated with some lesser scientist's child. But Rosemary will insist with an adamant shake of her head, showing, in the first smile that he will have seen from her for a long time, her big teeth. They're enough to frighten even taller men. ("But surely I'm entitled to. . . ." "Not yet," she will say.)

Before Rosemary goes to bed she pushes a message over the top of the barricaded attic door in which she explains the situation. She advises everyone to be dressed and ready for an early start the next morning and to have a big breakfast just in case, for one never knows, these days, if things will go as planned. She says that a bus is to be rented and that all of them, from the attic and basement alike, are to go off obediently to the Academy. It should be, she writes, pleasant for them to meet each other and for Basenji and Mary Ann to see their companions from the cages below again. And they should not worry; the time for action will come later. And would they please bring down with them all the Rosemary masks and dresses that are left in the attic as well as the several police uniforms they have rented.

CHAPTER XV
An Aristocrat

> The universe is truly in love with its
> task of fashioning whatever is next to
> be. . . .
>
> *Marcus Aurelius*

It is all very well to donate a group of females to the Academy of Motherhood, and one can only be commended for it, but if one of these creatures is wanted by the police as violent and dangerous, and another is under suspicion for intent to overthrow the civilized world, that is another story entirely. So what comes about is not quite what was expected.

The first part goes smoothly. John, now dressed as a clown, is, as they had hoped, considered by those at the Academy to be rapidly on his way to becoming a vulture, and therefore female. He is accepted without question, though of course John has *always* looked like a vulture; even as a child he had a long thin nose and glinting black eyes. He does not try to disillusion the Academy of Motherhood people, but deliberately walks with a jerky, avian motion. Also he has painted a vapid smile on his clown-face, knowing that if they feel superior to him they will be inclined to make snap judgments and not give him a second thought.

So it is that John is accepted along with the others, while Pooch/Isabel (complete with baby), and Rosemary (in the guise of her little-old-lady former self), and even the doctor (for harboring the other two) are, unfortunately, all three arrested and turned over to the police, along with all the Rosemary masks and dresses and police suits. One can understand this as far as Rosemary and Pooch are concerned, but the doctor? Perhaps the real reason for his arrest is that the members of the Academy do not want rivals off in their little corners making discoveries about motherhood on their own and so have turned him in to keep him from his research.

The Academy is happy to have a whole new set of creatures to experiment on, especially since one group of them has (except for the few hours running around town) already been kept isolated in an environment almost as sterile as their own. Here on the top floors, conditions are much as they were in the doctor's basement, except that they have the roof garden where they can sun themselves. This roof garden is scientific and has not been put there simply for the enjoyment of the mothers. It's well known that mothers-to-be and babies need plenty of vitamin D, so the roof has been made as pleasant as it possibly could be. Besides plants and potted trees, it contains a playground for the expected children with swings, slides, monkey bars, sandboxes, and mazes. The mothers-to-be have made good use of the playground themselves, and at no time, day or night, is it ever empty. The members of the Academy joke that the future mothers are trying to get their vitamin D by moonlight, but also feel that their suspicions of the degeneration of *all* females, whether on the way up or down, is confirmed by this behavior, for all the mothers indulge in it.

All those creatures that have been kept relatively germfree in the doctor's basement are scheduled for artificial insemination the day after tomorrow. The Academy uses only the best genes in the nation, those belonging to governors, generals (three star or above), atomic scientists, as well as those of the directors of nuclear reactors, presidents of the largest corporations, oil magnates, and so forth. The men picked are splendid, tall, and for the most part blonde. All earning well over $100,000 a year, not counting perks. Of course it has taken time for these men to achieve status in their fields, so most of them are by now paunchy and bald. (Since the imagination is suspect particularly at present, artists' and poets' genes are not used. Besides, it is hard to tell where artists come from. Some have dreadfully wizened little parents.)

★   ★   ★

Meanwhile, at the police station, there's a policeman who looks rather like a walrus, complete with mustache and honking voice. Another has arms like an ape and holds them as though waiting to grab somebody for some misdeed or other. One that looks like a giraffe, gun on heavy hip bone, is standing by the door. (It's always been this way, even before the women began their changes.) These three are questioning Pooch. Having seen that the doctor is alive and well except for a few scratches about the face and a small bandage on his neck, she is still dumbfounded at the good news that she is not a killer. She repeats over and over to herself, "I am not a dangerous animal," even though she knows that when she first came in she was booked as such.

In the next room she can hear the baby crying vigorously, in an absolute rage. Its crying is interspersed with growls and howls and fits of barking, mixed in with its small repertoire of words. Pooch thinks she hears several new ones, even two-word combinations like "bad man" and "go home" and "where's ma," plus one or two phrases quite unmentionable.

Now the policemen bring out a partially chewed old dog collar. She recognizes it instantly. It's in terrible shape and has an alien smell that she dislikes, which causes her to flinch away from it at first. Even so, they strap it around her neck, and in a strange way, having it there again is a wonderful relief. At least she now knows where she really lives and who she belongs to, and everyone else will know it too, at a glance. She feels almost as though she had slipped on a wedding ring. Perhaps she can relax now and let things take their course, and surely . . . surely *now* her master will come. What a joy it will be to see him again! At that thought she can hardly contain herself, and continuously wiggles about in the chair making little whining noises so that, what with the baby yelling, growling, and shouting obscenities in the next room and the doctor alive and well, it is impossible for Pooch to take in their questions. "Did you or did you not. . . ?" and so forth. She is nodding yes to everything.

And now they are reading off a long list of stolen articles: blue smock, golden key, sandals, heavy cream, smoked oysters, sprouts and nuts, jewelry, fruit, filet mignon, dog biscuits, balloon, pen, baby, scarves, paint rags, and, to top it all off, one pedigreed animal valued at over $600, registered with AKC as: Setter bitch. Show name: Astor's Empress Golden Eyes. Sire: Teasdale's Prince Tyrone. Dam: Astor's Empress Silver Fleece.

Who in the world is that? Pooch wonders. Golden Eyes!

They go on. "Said Golden Eyes, aka Isabel, aka Pooch."

Why, it's herself! She has stolen herself away, and worth over $600!

". . . irresponsible, dragging child through the gutter with no thought to its future . . . scantily dressed and up in a tree . . . subversive meeting, howling in the park. . . ." (As though she were the only one to blame for that!)

But $600! One could buy a decent car for that. Or a diamond. Pooch is stunned into stillness for a moment, but then the joy of being worth so much is added to the joy of being about to see her master. And now there is the joy of being able to give him back, not only his baby, but $600 worth of herself. Two valuable gifts indeed. But will he think she bit the baby? Why, of course not, for by now there's only a tiny scar. She herself has a hard time finding the place.

She gives a little moan. Nods yes and yes. The policemen have not the slightest idea that all this is a manifestation of joy. They have been warned by the doctor that this Pooch-Isabel-Golden Eyes is the most dangerous of all the animals in his care and that he always took precautions when dealing with her, that he knew she would one day attack him, that he had predicted the precise moment the attack would occur, and consequently was prepared for it and therefore not badly harmed. They diagnose her as hyperactive and wonder if her criminal behavior could be controlled with pills or a change of diet.

And now they have presented her with a written confession to sign. Pooch hesitates. What about Isabel's crimes? Isn't it Isabel who should be captured and incarcerated as an animal dangerous to society? But where does duty lie? And the master? What would make him most proud of her? Self-sacrifice for the sake of others? Surely that. Hasn't she been trained for it from the beginning? And to think of herself as last and least important? Trained to put-up-with? to acquiesce? to "stay" and "heel" and "sit" and "lie down and roll over?" Even though she sees that she might put a question into their minds by asking how she could have been, at the same time, at the Plaza and at the doctor's, she signs *yes* to everything. But she signs it in a sort of fit of exhilaration: *Pucci*. It's just as well that this is not her legal name.

★   ★   ★

In the halls on the way to her solitary confinement, Pooch sees several policemen wearing Rosemary masks. Most are still in their uniforms, though a few are wearing gray or navy blue dresses, their pistols and nightsticks making lumps under their skirts. She remembers the boxes of masks that had been confiscated at the Academy when the doctor and Pooch and Rosemary were arrested. There seems to be a lot of them. No doubt the police were already prepared to infiltrate the Rosemary movement. It's a little scary that one won't be able to know one's enemies for sure anymore, but even so Pooch gives little hops of joy.

In solitary, she calms down quickly and curls up on the floor by the door (though there is a cot in the cell) to await her master. The position doesn't seem quite as comfortable as it used to be. Perhaps she misses the scratchy mat, or perhaps her hip bones have broadened somewhat even in these last couple of weeks. She rests her cheek on one hand to keep it off the floor and with the other hand she fingers her worn-out collar.

"Not win," Rosemary had said to all of them just that morning, shortly before they had been separated from the others in the vestibule of the Academy of Motherhood. She had again been dressed as the little old Rosemary she used to be, and she had told them to remember that they were not trying to win. "And don't forget that," she said, "for if we do 'win' we will surely lose everything."

Pooch had not understood her. There, about to be arrested, and as strong and grand as she was under her gray dress, she had said, "Not win." But now, thinking of her master and the pleasures of duty, Pooch decides she does understand. Of course there is nothing to win . . . nothing but someone else's love. And to be loyal to it. Loyalty! That is, after all, what she was born for, and how satisfying it is to still be so. How relaxing, to lean back (loyally) into someone else's love and care, never to want to win anything ever again.

She begins to compose in her mind a joyful and nostalgic haiku:

Daisies, dish soap, doormat,
smell of his chair.
Oh breath of golden spring!

(She had especially wanted to work the word *golden* into it.)

There is barely time to count syllables and she knows it needs much more work, though she does like the middle line. Her solitary confinement hardly lasts half an hour when the baby, still screaming and furious, is brought to her. Obviously the policemen can no longer deal with its noise. She had been a little worried about it, but had known that when the master came, all would be well with them both. Still, it's a relief to take it into her arms, where it stops yelling instantly and turns from beet red to its normal peachy glow. For the last few days the two of them have had so little time to enjoy each other. Ever since the time she and Basenji had curled up together for comfort. So now she is happy to have a chance to get reacquainted with it. With some bits of rag from her skirt (which makes the skirt all the more disreputable), she forms a ball for the baby to throw and for herself to fetch. The baby screaming again, but now with delight.

A few hours later the master does come. Pooch knows who it is even before the door opens — that special beer and pipe tobacco, that armpit smell that could only be *his* armpits. Stronger now than ever. Probably because he no longer has

Pooch to do his laundry. Yes, that will be the first thing she'll do for him.

The door slams open and Pooch leaps into his arms and begins kissing his cheeks . . . his whole face. She nearly knocks him over. In her joy a word does come out — "Master." Just once. And Pooch is even more ecstatic to find her voice returning, however hoarse and gravelly it sounds. But then she is shocked to silence again when he leans her over backward, puts his hand up under her paint smock to one of her breasts, and gives her a long French kiss — not at all fatherly. She pulls away from him as soon as he loosens his grip slightly. Can this be her master? The man from whom she learned, or thought she had learned, all her upstanding loyalty and morality, though perhaps she had made it all up out of her own needs. All of a sudden she wonders — where *did* she learn them? From the operas, no doubt, and the haiku. Or Bernard Meltzer. And has she ever really known the master, for here in his hand, a chain, a choke collar, a short whip, handcuffs, and a muzzle. Muzzle! Clearly he has been convinced that she is a dangerous animal, in spite of all that he knows of her. Why, she grew up with him! How can he think this about her? How can he kiss her in that way? Like the sybarite's kiss only, actually, more violent and less sensuous . . . not sensuous at all, in fact, a cruel and frightening kiss.

"You're to come home," he says. "I told them I'd keep you in line. From what I hear of your recent experiences, you already know very well where bad animals go and what happens to them there. I hope you can keep that in your head. I left the laundry. The houseplants died. Be careful and we'll both have a real good time. My wife, as you must realize, is now at the aquarium, so *if* things go well, I thought we might get married later on."

He motions for her to pick up the baby. Then, when it is in her arms, he gives it a peck on the cheek, but pulls back with a yell. There are red teeth marks at the side of his upper lip. The baby has bitten him.

CHAPTER XVI
A Daring Escape

> Alas, I cast my nets into their seas and
> wanted to catch good fish; but I always
> pulled up the head of some old god.
> *Friedrich Nietzsche*

By now, in a manner of speaking, all men have lost their mothers. Even if the mothers still live where they have always lived, they are grayer or greener than expected or more mustachioed. They slide down banisters, fall asleep on the Persian rug in front of the fireplace, and, rain or shine, dance around in the back yard (if there is a back yard); otherwise, on the roof. They smile at nothing or at anything or are always almost smiling. Talk about the Mona Lisa! Others do not encounter their mothers except on outings to the zoo. Some mothers have not been seen at all for quite some time, and the worst is feared.

Of course all the members of the Academy are disturbed by the loss of or changes in their own mothers. Many have always treated their mothers with the utmost kindness and consideration, carrying their suitcases, opening doors and jars, and reaching into high places for them. They regret — especially now, and considering their own recent losses or problems with their mothers — they regret that circumstances have forced them to lock away, virtually imprison these other younger mothers, along with a few older, more experienced ones.

A large room at the Academy has been set apart for the use of the members. A moose head hangs on one wall, tiger, wildebeest, and assorted deer and antelope on the others. There is a bear skin on the floor and near it a zebra skin. A cut-off elephant foot stands by the door as a receptacle for canes and umbrellas. It is to this room that the members of the Academy often come to discuss their own mothers and mothers in general. No female is ever allowed in, except once a week a small, blotchy one in a black uniform is let in to clean up.

At the exact moment that Pooch is running out from between her master's legs (this time, in truth, knocking him over) — she is holding the baby in her teeth by the back of its diaper — at that exact moment the little blotchy female enters this room, and in a few minutes out comes a zebra, walking upright with a wildebeest head in its forefeet. Ten minutes later the same thing happens, except that this time out comes a bear with two antelope heads in its paws.

There are no members in the members' room because today is a big day at the Academy. Not only is there the excitement of all the new mothers-to-be just brought in, but the first babies (twins, actually) to be born under completely scientific observation, from insemination on, are about to be delivered. True, they have not taken nine months to gestate, but who can tell how long is normal now that things have changed so much. And anyway, twins are often a bit premature. Two heartbeats have been clearly heard and two skeletons seen on the x-rays. One member of the Academy is even sure that he heard three heartbeats and that three little skeletons are quite easily seen if one looks properly.

The donor of the sperm of these particular infants is a man high up in government circles. His identity of course is a secret, but it is known that he was handsome in his younger years, he has already fathered several successful males, and he once played football. The members of the Academy have great expectations for these babies. Their future has been mapped out for them already.

Several Academy members are dressed in their operating room greens and the contractions are coming every five minutes. Many of the mothers-to-be who have expressed an interest are allowed to watch the procedure. It is hoped that they will learn something useful. They stand behind the Academy members, up on boxes so that they can see over the members' shoulders. They are being unusually quiet.

But soon there is as much confusion and consternation at the Academy as there is at the police station. At first no one is quite sure what has happened. What sort of baby is this? . . . this naked, shapeless lump, almost all head? Perhaps it is an extra-large rat . . . or pig, or pup? Could be anything—don't they all look like this in the beginning? But certainly . . . or *almost* certainly not human, though hairless enough. Pig. Probably pig. And goodness knows how many more to come, yet from a creature obviously on the way up and with only the slightest suggestion of the porcine about her. And wasn't she thought to be "up" from racehorse and by Secretariat? She is still in labor, but now no one is paying any attention to her except Cucumber (Pickle for short), who has been holding her hand all this time and wiping her face with a cool, damp cloth. (The members of the Academy not only allow such behavior, they encourage it. Besides, they are concentrating on the important end.)

It is at this moment of confusion, when the Academy members have just turned to stare at each other in astonishment, that all the mothers-to-be (Chloe and Phillip among them) spring into action and fall—literally fall from the vantage of their higher perches—upon the members of the Academy and, by dint of their numbers and the element of surprise, easily overpower them.

(Cucumber had snatched the new baby out of harm's way in the nick of time.)

First the mothers-to-be take away all the Academy members' keys and then they hustle them down to the baby paraphernalia shop. Cucumber doesn't mind staying with the mother, who is still in labor. She has never been interested in anything athletic and actually prefers to stay behind. She is hoping that the next baby born will be something quite different from the first—that would be an adventure of its own sort.

Down in the shop, there are unfortunately only three Responsive Early-Life Play Pens. Chloe and Phillip help the others pick out from the group of green-clad and business-suited men the three who seem the most important. They do this partly by an examination of their underwear (whether it was bought at JC

Penney's or not) and partly by who the men defer to. After they put the three men in the pens, they load the dispenser with the nutrition cupcakes (also on sale there) and punch in the proper program—they pick one that is for particularly recalcitrant children, good for either the terrible twos or the frustrating fives. They are hoping that with some positive reinforcement, as well as a modicum of negative reinforcement, these most important members of the Academy can be reprogrammed to behave in a way that is more sensitive to the needs of all creatures. Perhaps after a day in the pens, they will have switched sides.

The men will not be badly off. They will be rocked and sung to. Educational stories will be read to them by soft voices. When they need to pee, they will afterward be air-dried and powdered. After some time they may even learn to enjoy it, though now there isn't much else for them to do *but* enjoy it as best they can. Of course they will also have plenty of time to think about the pig-baby (if such it really is).

The rest of the members of the Academy are confined with various sorts of baby paraphernalia—straps, harnesses, and leashes—and given pills for hyperactive children. Then the mothers-to-be return to the roof, where all the other mothers and former mothers have gathered and where John is practicing his juggling and back flips. They stop on the way up, however, in the rest-and-relaxation room, where they take all the remaining animal heads off the walls, even including the moose head, which is so heavy it takes three of them to carry it. These they bring with them to the roof garden.

*   *   *

Pooch is stopped, of course. Right away. She is no sooner out the door than she is grabbed by a very large policeman. He was standing there as though waiting for her, and he is the largest policeman she has ever seen. And fat, too. He holds her arm so tightly that she can feel all four fingers and thumb, and she knows she'll have five bruises from it. "It's me," the policeman keeps whispering to her. "It's me, it's me. Me!" And all the while he is dragging her to the back of the building instead of toward the front door where she is struggling to go. She is struggling so hard to escape that she hardly hears what he's saying and doesn't even pay attention to her nose, for there is certainly a strong, musky smell to this policeman . . . a hot, damp fur smell. The baby, all this while, is trying to bite the policeman, but can't get a grip on anything but cloth. But then it does get a grip on rubber and the policeman's hand seems to tear away, showing long white glistening fur and the tips of five (abominable) black fingers visible beneath it. As with every human being, it is by now the visual that strikes Pooch the most forcefully, rather than the aural or olfactory.

Clearly Rosemary, hunching down and disguised as her lumpy old self, has overpowered a policeman (a large one), traded clothes with him, and left him, perhaps in the very cell where he had been about to lock her up.

So now Pooch lets herself be led to a back room, with the baby still trying to bite Rosemary, though Pooch is struggling to keep it turned away. She's worried that the baby will be biting all the time now just to cause some excitement, since that first bite at the side of the master's lip was so effective and made so much happen. Poor baby. Pooch wonders not only what will become of it, but what it will become. And then that bite that had started off all these misadventures, when the baby was bitten by its own mother. But for that they'd never have left home. Though now . . . of course the master is under a lot of tension, but it's clear that home is not what it used to be.

And here he is now, the master, as though a reminder of how it really is and perhaps was all along. He has come up behind them and is beating Pooch with the short whip. It is of braided leather with four short tails, hardly longer than two feet. He is beating at her face and shoulders with all his strength, yelling that she must be retrained and that he paid over six hundred dollars for her. Already there are red welts on the back of her neck and on her cheek, but Pooch is so angry that the lashes don't hurt. She is holding her arms and hands over the baby to protect it rather than over her own head (she still has the back of its diaper in her teeth) and is wondering, how can the master endanger his own baby like this? Why there is even a red mark, now, on its cheek. Luckily another policeman, coming down the hall in the opposite direction, misinterprets the situation, pulls the master away, easily takes the whip from him, and leads him off toward the front of the building. Pooch can hear the master yelling all the way: "You're making a mistake. That animal just bit me right here. By the lip. Has killed."

Pooch is so angry at the lie that she hopes the baby *does* bite everyone it sees — and she may do the same. She wonders if she, too, had a mother who bit. That is certainly possible, though considering her pedigree it's unlikely. I am a dangerous animal, she thinks, and proud of it. But Rosemary's grip on her arm reminds her that her strength is only the strength of an ordinary female human being, that her humanity will force her to use her wits instead, and that she must now try to live by the mind. All right, she thinks, whether *some* human beings are acting human or not, I will do so, and do so proudly. And he called *me* animal!

So, led by Rosemary, she marches off to a back room where three policemen are interrogating the doctor. As soon as the baby sees him it begins to shout "Poo poo" and "Go away." Then it pushes itself out of Pooch's arms (Pooch lets go of the diaper in her teeth) and, actually standing up, the baby wobbles towards the doctor, mouth open, ready to take a bite. Unfortunately, it seems that the baby has somehow, in spite of the lack of opportunities to practice, and here, at the worst possible moment, learned to walk.

"Go away, little boy," one of the policemen says, though not unkindly. Probably because the baby is still completely bald — only a fine, almost colorless see-through fuzz on the top of its head — the policeman has taken it for a male. Or perhaps it is the vicious look in its eye that makes him think so.

But now Rosemary is holding her furry white hand in front of them all, and Pooch is standing beside her with her own kind of grin, teeth bared, looking rather like the baby had a moment before.

The policemen, all three, whip out their guns and tell Rosemary to take off her stolen police uniform and mask, to turn around, and "up-against-the-wall." She doesn't turn around, but slowly takes off the uniform and mask, all the while looking at the three policemen in turn. They watch, fascinated, as the whole of Rosemary appears, shimmering in all her abominable brilliance. They are so absorbed that the doctor, the baby, and Pooch aren't noticed. They move as though on signal, though there is no signal. The doctor, handcuffed with his hands behind him, butts his head into the back of the policeman in front of him. Pooch jumps on the one in the middle. The baby has by now reached the doctor and firmly bites his ear so that Rosemary can, with one swipe of her big arm, cause all three of them to drop their guns. But the baby will not let go of the doctor's ear. Pooch thinks again of its mother and quickly resorts to the same solution that she used in that case: a lit match to the chin. The baby lets go in order to bark at her. This time the barking is a relief to Pooch. At least it shows that the baby cannot be becoming all snapping turtle. In fact, Pooch believes that its ability to speak (as now it is saying "Don't" and "No"), *and* bark, *and* bite, *and* growl, *and* walk, *and* crawl, all surely confirm that it is remaining human, although no doubt a little perverted by its experiences. One would hope not irreversibly so.

One of these days, if she does not end up in jail for good, Pooch hopes to be able to make a happy home for the baby, now that the other home is completely out of the question (and now that becoming an opera star seems unlikely, though she had once hoped to be able to combine career and marriage and perhaps even to bear children of her own).

★ ★ ★

By now the policemen, gagged and wearing nothing but their undershorts, are handcuffed to each other and to the heating pipe in the far corner of the room. Rosemary is back in her policeman's suit, and Pooch and the doctor, free of the handcuffs, are also dressed as policemen. Rosemary has put the guns, clubs, and walkie-talkies into a plastic bag that she found in the waste-basket. The doctor had wanted to keep the guns and clubs, and Pooch was tempted too, wanting to have something with which to defend the baby from the doctor, though she is more occupied, right now, with the opposite problem. She still does not quite understand how the doctor came to be on their side and why she should be escaping now with the very person who deprived her of her voice. But Rosemary has easily wrested the gun from her. "Don't be silly. You're not going to kill anyone and I don't believe you ever have."

Rosemary bundles up the third policeman's uniform and tucks it under her arm. "Come on," she says, "or we'll miss the main action." She will drop the bag with the guns and clubs into the first sewer they pass, and give the uniform to the first outrageous female it fits.

CHAPTER XVII
In Which the Baby Saves Itself

Whither, 'midst falling dew,
  While glow the heavens with the last
  steps of day,
Far, through their rosey depths, dost
  thou pursue
Thy solitary way?
William Cullen Bryant

There are not many vestiges left to Isabel of the human being she had once been: a random word or two, the coquettish way she behaves when in sight of anything male, a gold bracelet that she keeps simply because she has forgotten how to release the catch. She lost her bearings long ago, though she still circles the Waldorf Astoria (but of course avoids the Plaza; she has that much sense). She still looks in Altman's and Lord and Taylor's windows, and can often be found around three AM drinking from the fountain at Lincoln Center (popular watering hole for many of the female creatures in the early morning hours). Sometimes she balances on her hind legs, showing off her black fur coat and the white patch on her chest. If anyone approaches, lured by her sporadically provocative behavior, she warns them away with a show of teeth. Touchy, suspicious, always alone, but now a creature-mildness shows in her eyes. She will kill, but only if cornered. When she was more human, one was never quite sure what she was capable of. The temperament of a wolverine has made her, if anything, a little *less* wild — for the first time, willing to let well enough alone. In her present state, no one would wish harm to her in spite of what she has done, but only that she should be removed safely to Montana or upper Michigan.

Isabel usually sleeps until noon, as was her habit before all these changes began, but today something has awakened her earlier than usual. A rustling in the trees and on the ground, twitterings and laughter. She sees all sorts of female creatures gathering in small groups and combining into larger ones. Everyone is heading south. Isabel follows, keeping a safe distance. It is clear that she still has vestiges of that insatiable human trait, curiosity.

★ ★ ★

Valdoviccini, consumed with longing not only for the throaty baying voice he had heard from the top balcony a few weeks ago, but also for Chloe — especially for Chloe — has spent the night wandering in the vicinity of his Village *pied-à-terre*. He has found that he has more feelings for Chloe than he had thought. In fact more feelings for her than he has had for anyone in a long time, perhaps ever. Unlike all the women he has known before, she never minded his idiosyncracies, was neither afraid of him nor condemned him. Always she remained aloof, always sinuous and elegant, always dignified in *any* position. He remembers her curled up on the windowsill as though waiting for him. She would blink at him. Then stretch. Such a voluptuous stretch! In the garbage, for she cleaned up after herself (another aspect he liked about her: always impeccable), he would find the empty cartons of cream, the empty jars of caviar, the shells of the frozen shrimp he'd bought her. She was a voluptuous eater, and he liked that about her, too. Voluptuous in other ways — in *all* ways (like him in that) for, now and then, she would be so sexually turned on that she would roll on the floor and yowl. He knew she was disturbing the neighbors, but he didn't care. That black face! Those blue eyes! He doesn't want any other face than that one. Even the way they fought, a childish bickering they both enjoyed. And yet he has never told her that he liked her . . . loved. . . . But she must have seen that. Though why should she, when he hadn't even seen it himself?

Now he is wondering — and the thought terrifies him — if she could have been rounded up and taken to the Academy to be inseminated. If it's not too late, maybe he can persuade them that he should be the one to father her child. He is, after all, well known in his field. Also he is well paid. He will go, now, to the

Academy and see if she is there and, if she is, he will do anything to get her back or, if that can't be, to father her child. He does not let himself think that she might have been taken instead to the pound, though in the back of his mind he knows that, if she is not at the Academy of Motherhood, he will rush to the pound. He hopes they are still required by law to keep the inmates seven days. Before he leaves he puts that cryptic note in his pocket: "I am she whom you seek."

★ ★ ★

The streets are full of policemen and Rosemarys—probably exactly what Rosemary had in mind when she brought down the masks and uniforms from the attic. Some of the Rosemarys are very large indeed while many of the policemen are quite small and have rolled-up pants legs that keep coming down and tripping them. Now and again there is a car that has hit a lamppost or fire hydrant and has not yet been towed away, or that has stopped right in the middle of the street. None of the policemen pays the slightest attention to them.

★ ★ ★

Rosemary, the doctor, Pooch, and the baby have no sooner hurried away from the police station than they see a group of Rosemarys on the opposite street corner looking at them and speaking into their walkie-talkies. Rosemary leads Pooch and the doctor in a quick right turn down a side street, but the other Rosemarys make that same turn and follow, half a block behind. Pooch is too busy to think about this, though; she is having a great deal of trouble keeping the baby from biting the doctor again. He tells Pooch, "That baby should get out of your sphere of influence before it is damaged irrevocably." He has called her Isabel twice and 107 three times already.

Again Pooch is wondering how (or if) the doctor got to be on their side. He had represented the essence of evil to her because he thought only of ends and never seemed to consider means or meals. She is wondering how it came about that they are trotting down the street together as though the dreadful testing that went on in the laboratory had never taken place. But Rosemary seems to have him under control.

In answer to the doctor Pooch shakes her head vigorously, but he isn't looking. Then she manages to bark out a fairly clear "No," which the baby reiterates. In the same barking fashion, she stutters, "Not, not, not, not. . . ." And at last she gets out a fairly clear "Isabel." Barks, yes, but a "Not Isabel" nonetheless. But the effort is wasted. She is walking a bit behind the other two, for the safety of the doctor, and just as she manages to get the words out, she trips on her unrolling pants and falls down. Since she is behind them, the others don't notice and hurry on.

Behind Pooch come those other Rosemarys. Quickly she slips completely out of her hopelessly entangled policeman pants. Thank goodness the policeman's jacket comes down almost to her knees. With the baby in her teeth again, she runs off down an alley as fast as she can. One of the Rosemarys leaves the others and follows her. It seems to Pooch that the Rosemarys could have easily caught up with her when she fell, but apparently following her is more important than arresting her. Perhaps that was why it was so easy to leave the police station. Perhaps they were let go on purpose.

★　★　★

It happens that in this particular alley a kazoo, tom-tom, and tambourine band has been gathering, getting ready to march up Fifth Avenue. There are several Rosemarys as well as several policemen in the band. Also many females in various states of change, the most impressive being a large, kazooing condor-woman. What's left of her orange hair (it is clear she will soon be completely bald) blends in with her orange head. Her arms are covered already with black feathers, a strip of white ones on each side. Pooch thinks how nice that such endangered species can now augment their ranks with changing females.

The kazoo band is about to move out. As Pooch and the Rosemary near them, the kazoo players accept them into their ranks and hand them (the baby, too) kazoos and invite them to line up. There is really little else to do, since the alley has turned out to be a dead end.

The baby is delighted and so is Pooch, because here is a way for her to sing again, however harsh the sound. And so Pooch and the baby, side by side with the Rosemary who has been following them, march out with the others toward, Pooch hopes, whatever it is that Rosemary said they should hurry up for.

Then, right in the middle of all this new-found pleasure, she catches sight of Isabel, crouching behind a pile of plastic trash bags. How not stop and greet her, even though Pooch would rather go on marching with the kazoo group? Clearly Isabel had not gone to the master as Pooch had advised, though that is probably just as well. Now no way to ask her, nor has Isabel the means to reply.

The Rosemary has stopped also, but stands at a discreet distance as Pooch approaches and squats down, holding out her hand, palm up. Isabel moves forward cautiously and touches the tip of her nose to the tips of Pooch's fingers. She is looking at Pooch's collar as though once again her salvation lies in that. To her it must mean freedom, as it did back at the pound.

To Pooch the collar has come to mean a sort of slavery. Disgusting thing! Why had she not taken it off at the first opportunity? Now, in her eagerness to do so, she lets go of the squirming baby and it toddles off as fast as it can after the kazoo band, calling out, "Mine, mine." Falls down. Gets up. Falls. . . .

Pooch hands the collar to Isabel, who takes it tentatively, making little grunts of pleasure. Then Isabel turns back to the nearest doorway and begins to chew on it. Pooch thinks that now the collar is being used as it deserves to be.

Pooch turns to find the Rosemary making off with the baby, and she rushes after them. But no need to hurry, for the baby, it seems, has learned, in just this half day, to defend itself. The Rosemary yells and drops it and the baby crawls off as fast as it can, still after the kazoo group, having for the moment given up on walking.

Pooch grabs the baby with one hand and then turns to see where the Rosemary was bitten. It is quite a bad bite on the hand. Pooch looks closely at the baby, trying to see any changes toward the animal in the set of its jaw or its teeth, but they seem the normal chubby chin and sharp little teeth of any human baby. "Mine," it says again, reaching after the kazoo band and waving its fingers. It is quite flushed, and Pooch thinks perhaps she should look for some water for it, but there is the bite to deal with first. There is a handkerchief in the top part of her policeman's uniform that could be used as a bandage. She holds back her instinct to lick the wound (though she once read that that is a good thing to do) and carefully wipes away the blood with the cleanest part of the handkerchief.

"*That* is Isabel," the Rosemary says in a gravelly, bass voice. A nice voice, actually. Pooch is drawn to it. The Rosemary is nodding toward Isabel, who is still chewing away noisily.

"I'm the detective who was called to the Plaza. I expect that is the real Isabel. That's the one that killed the cook, not you."

Pooch can see the detective's eyes behind his Rosemary mask. They are blue and have little wrinkles at the sides, and she can even see dark circles underneath them. They are performing the wound-binding like a ritual; he is helping her with his left hand since she must hold the baby, and she is as gentle as she can be. Each using just one hand, they tie the knot at the end.

Perhaps the kazooing has loosened something in Pooch's throat. Or perhaps it was the giving away of the collar, as if: There goes home and all it stands for. No turning back. Rely, now, only on yourself. (She wonders, does she have the courage?)

"I have not spoken for several days, though I have felt the need," Pooch says as their fingers touch. She had not thought that she was about to speak. Her voice takes her by surprise. It is soft and pure and full of humanity, and there is no trace of a stutter. One could say it's better than ever.

"You know you shouldn't have confessed to all those crimes

back at the police station. You shouldn't have signed that statement."

"My voice was taken from me by a mad scientist who, though he conceived of himself as kindly and no doubt still thinks so, used me viciously, trying to wrest from me secrets I never possessed."

"No doubt," the detective says, "he was concerned about the future of motherhood. We all are, you know."

"I have always hoped to be a mother one day." The baby, suddenly worn out, is leaning against Pooch's shoulder, breathing quietly into its kazoo. As though to illustrate her feelings, Pooch gives it a little lick on the cheek.

"Mothering well, as you seem to be doing, is all well and good," the detective says, "but the state of motherhood in general involves the entire planet."

"I know I must not think that *'una voce poco fa,'*" says Pooch.

"But come, let's get you some decent clothes. You look disgraceful in that policeman's jacket and almost nothing else. You'll give the force a bad name."

CHAPTER XVIII
A New Wardrobe

Change is nature's delight.
Marcus Aurelius

The entire planet wavers in its orbit. Mysterious star-forces bombard it. For a few minutes the sky looks as if it's full of northern lights, even though it's daytime. There's lightning now and then, but no clouds. Everyone on the street is dizzy from looking up. People bump into each other. The light is so particularly strong right over the Academy of Motherhood that everyone is wondering who has been born there this morning. What would they think if they knew it was three piglets and a colt? Probably they would wonder if the colt would one day win the Preakness.

The city seems free of pollution. Con Ed has shut down, perhaps because there's so much electricity in the air already. (One should not worry about the safety of the three important men confined to the Responsive Early-Life Play Pens. The pens have self-contained, fail-safe electrical units, advertised as safe for as long as two months after an atomic blast. Of course they're so expensive that only upper-class children could afford to be saved.) Most of the cars and trucks are stuck at the edges of the city because the wildebeests have been kind enough to turn back from their migration and help their sisters by keeping traffic in a snarl outside the city limits. Anyone who wants to come in must walk or ride on some creature, if they can find one willing to accept them. The air smells fresh, enigmatic, earthy, slightly sour — almost like the very stuff of females — outlandish and uncanny.

George (for the detective has now introduced himself), Pooch, and the baby have reached Lincoln Center. Pooch recognizes it at once, with a little frisson of excitement. She gestures towards the New York City Opera. She whispers. She is still not sure her voice will be there when she wants it and what she is about to say, she hardly dares venture. "Perhaps it is here," she says, "I might find some decent clothes." Of course she is thinking of clothes that would be much more than decent. She is thinking of something Carmen would be wearing at Lellas Pastia's tavern.

Since George is a detective with badge, it isn't hard for him to get access to places. "Why not?" the doorman says leading them in. "Half the costumes are gone already. All of *La Traviata*, gone. And Gilda, Aïda, Susanna, Santuzza, Mimi. . . . The divas themselves took lots of them. I didn't dare stop them." He is a chickadeelike man, soft and plump. One does not wonder that he was afraid, considering all those brand-new claws, hooves, incisors, and beaks he probably had to deal with.

The costume room has been well picked over. Pooch looks first for third-act *Carmen* costumes, but all the gypsy clothes are gone. Then something feathery catches her eye. At the end of a far rack . . . a complete bird suit! Papagena! No one would ever recognize her in that. There's a feathered cap of iridescent green and purple, which changes color at every tiny move. It fits low over her ears and forehead. Also a matching bodice and a short, feathered skirt that turns up into a tail behind. All the feathers in it are curled and downy and mostly reds and oranges. Then there are yellow leggings that show off her nice new long legs. Everything fits as though it had been made especially for her. She has never felt so gaily dressed.

She is so elated that a haiku pops into her head practically in finished form:

What if every creature were part bird?
Could fly, glitter, whistle?
Topknot on head! Red!

Of course she doesn't really want to be a bird. She knows that it is the human being who can pretend to be anything, and she will never, now, give up being human. What other creature could have invented opera and haiku? Of course they also invented war and pollution, but perhaps it all goes together, the best and the worst. Maybe it's animalness that will make the world right again: the wisdom of elephants, the enthusiasm of canines, the grace of snakes, the mildness of anteaters. Perhaps being human needs some diluting. At any rate, how nice to be well dressed and among friends and in a state where poems pop out by themselves.

George and the doorman both break into spontaneous applause at the sight of her, but the baby is terrified and will not be comforted, until a satin Cherubino jacket is pinned around it and it is given a large feather to hold along with its kazoo.

All four of them, the doorman included, now head for Fifty-seventh Street.

CHAPTER XIX
She Whom He Seeks

> And I say unto you: one must still have
> chaos in oneself to be able to give birth
> to a dancing star.
>
> *Friedrich Nietzsche*

The forces of motherhood have had to set up pro tem headquarters in an inferior building across the street from the Academy now that the Academy has been taken over by the mothers-to-be. Even though three vice presidents of motherhood and several important scientists and officials of motherhood have been captured, there are plenty of members of the Academy still at large. It is these who are now gathered across the street to consider their alternatives. They are wondering if they should, perhaps, abandon motherhood altogether . . . at least the sort of motherhood that has anything to do with females. How unfortunate that they have, until now, been dependent on women for filling their *own* ranks. But science must triumph. They are saying, if a hill is in our way as we build a road, nowadays we have only to remove it. Mountains even. If great valleys need to be crossed, we build equally great bridges. Why not simply sidestep the female? We've already been doing this, to a lesser extent, for generations. And it worked — as far as it went. We've made invisible those who were less like us than they might be. We will build a higher bridge. To ignore them will be their greatest defeat. It always has been.

But one of the members says they should, on the contrary, confront the females. How would they know they were brave if they didn't face the women head on? Another of the members wonders if the females — especially those who are leaders and winners — shouldn't be allowed to become honorary men, with all the rights and privileges that that entails.

143

One has secretly gone down into the basement to make pipe bombs.

★ ★ ★

Now the city seems one big parade, with everyone converging on Fifty-seventh Street. There is music of all sorts: whistling, beeping, and tootling. Even the night creatures have come up into the day to see what's going on and to contribute their chirps, hoots, and loon-laughter. They wear dark glasses and their hats are pulled low over their eyes, but still they walk proudly with the others.

Suddenly, high above it all, a coloratura cadenza can be heard, clearly a trained voice, and only a little higher than a normal human voice could go. The "Bell Song" from *Lakmé*, and here comes a group of opera singers on a float pulled by two huge Clydesdale mares. Each mare wears a wide-brimmed blue floppy hat and a flowered shawl. Their tails are neatly braided, as are their manes. They pull willingly. One can see they are happy to be able to make this contribution to females, to the opera, and to the circus. It is now, just at the end of the aria, that Pooch hears "Pa." Tentative. Questioning. "Pa?" She does not dare answer. "Pa?" Where is this "pa" coming from? As yet Pooch can see nothing of the float and its occupants. Besides, can she still sing? Does she dare to try?

"Pa!" This time it is prolonged, insistent, demanding. "Paaaaa!"

Then she sees the float, and the feathered crest looping up above the others, and she feels a tingle of anticipation. Silly, she thinks, one chicken attracted to another. She promises herself she will not be again misled as she was by the Escamillo, falling in love with an imaginary person . . . with a role. No, not again in love with a costume.

Then the creature leaps off the float, pa-ing vigorously, and comes straight to her. The crowd opens up for him. And such a tall, bright thing he is! "Pa." She sings it tentatively, not knowing what will happen, but it comes out so full-throated that everyone turns to stare at her. "Pa," again. And again. And he, his pale eyes. . . . They *are* the same pale eyes—the very ones! Yes, and the Escamillo voice. She'd recognize it anywhere. They laugh and begin to sing the duet as it should be sung. Even as they are singing, many hands pull them up onto the wagon full of opera singers. Here she is at last, she and the baby, among them. Then she sees, just beyond, a fat and familiar mustachioed face . . . a too-familiar face, and he is calling out to her, "Wait, wait. You are she whom I seek." She turns away. Of course he doesn't recognize her in this costume. No one does. Probably not even the pale young man, though she is hoping that he does, now, as he holds her elbow and looks into her eyes.

"I, also, was seeking you," the young man says. "Yes, it really is you, and I see that you know me. And I knew you weren't that old woman back then when I went for another balloon. First I recognized the baby, but then I could see that it was you by your eyes. I've remembered your eyes ever since the stage door . . . your golden-brown eyes. I'll always know who you are from them."

Pooch is human enough by now to blush at his words. The transparent down on her cheeks (hardly as much as on the baby's head) cannot hide it. She also cannot hide her smile of pleasure.

But now the little orchestra on the float has begun the familiar strains, and the young man takes her hand. "Do you know this aria?"

Of course she does; it's Carmen's "bird" song: "Love, like a rebellious bird." How apropos! To the costume, at least. And he is leading her to the front of the platform. "Come, sing a solo."

Here they are at Fifty-seventh Street. And there, right in front of the Academy of Motherhood building, things have been arranged as though for a circus, or perhaps for an extraordinarily acrobatic opera. High wires have been stretched, and trapezes and huge nets guyed from buildings and street lights. A ringmaster, in top hat and white riding breeches, stands beside a similarly attired dwarf. Both are full-breasted women. Several clowns of both sexes are already doing skits to keep the crowd happy before the real show begins.

But that particular Academy member who had gone into the basement for his nefarious purpose has come up with a large shopping bag. He makes his way through the crowd and crosses the street with his heavy load. He has never been the most reasonable of the members, though he was one of those who had always been particularly nice to his mother.

CHAPTER XX
A Catastrophe

> Everything worth while in him had
> come from mankind. . . . His love of
> the arts, of wisdom, of the 'humanities'!
> God! Would that wisdom lay rather in
> 'caninities'!
>
> *Olaf Stapledon*

Pooch's voice has always gathered crowds and either made them silent or set them to humming along. Now all the creatures near her fall silent, the thousands of false Rosemarys and false policemen as well as those, male and female, who are simply being themselves. Even the kazoo band, almost a block away, changes its tune so that it can hum along in harmony with her singing. Pooch's way of singing has changed the meaning of the aria. It has become contemplative and seems to be saying something sad about them all. *"Quand je vous aimerai? . . . Peut-être jamais, . . . L'oiseau rebelle . . . c'est bien en vain qu'on l'appelle. . . . L'oiseau que tu croyais surprendre, battit de l'aile et s'envola; . . ."* Why, it's not the bird of love at all, but the bird of life. At those words, *"batite de l'aile,"* Pooch makes little helpless flapping gestures. How can anyone not love this small, fluttering Papagena! She brings to every mind a new thought of what love and life might be. If her master had been there in the crowd, surely he, too, would have changed for the better, if only for the duration of the song.

When Pooch has finished, the pale young man grabs her and hugs her so as to quite crush her feathers, and the crowd yells "Encore, encore." Valdoviccini has pushed to the front and is standing just below her, yelling as loud as any of the others.

Looking him right in the eye and still safely enfolded in the arms of her Papageno, Pooch removes her feathered cap and lets her silky ears hang down.

"No," he shouts, "it can't be!" But she nods, yes.

147

"I've been a fool," he says, but then he surprises her. "Oh," (and there is such pain in his voice) "where is Chloe? I must find her and, dear Pucci, please forgive me, and do you think Chloe ever will?"

He looks so desperate that Pooch believes he is sincere. He might still be thoughtless and selfish, perhaps ignorant (or, more likely, too wise in worldly ways and not ignorant enough), but not actually cruel. Of course the same might be said about the doctor and his dreadful experiment. Perhaps he also was thoughtless and too knowledgeable. Perhaps even the master. . . .

Well, why should she be the judge and jury of such things? "The last I saw Chloe," she says, "she was there," and she points, at the Academy of Motherhood. "She and a number of others donated themselves for the motherhood experiments. I would be among them if I had not been taken away."

Just as they turn toward the building, the bombs go off.

First the front doors burst outward in smoke and flying glass. A few seconds later flames are seen deeper inside. Perhaps some of the paraphernalia, regalia, and insignia of motherhood are not as fireproof as advertised. (One cannot help but wonder if this is on purpose, or if some antimotherhood forces have infiltrated the promotherhood staff, or if the motherhood staff itself may have more ambiguous feelings than one would have wished.) At any rate, a fire is well under way and as soon as the two primary blasts go off, other blasts follow.

Creatures scurry hither and yon, some pushing back away from the blaze, others pushing forward toward it. Pooch can see, silhouetted against the smoke and flames, creatures hurrying to rescue those trapped inside. Rosemary in her policeman suit looms above all of them, pushing her way into the building. She is followed by the doctor, also in policeman outfit, and after him by several Rosemarys, pulling their skirts up and tucking them inside their policeman pants at the waist. And then Valdoviccini. Pooch wonders how he got to the doors so fast in all this confusion, and after him . . . goodness, Isabel! What possesses her to enter that inferno? Can she actually want to rescue someone?

Then Pooch, without a second thought, rushes to the fiery doorway. She doesn't know what is in her mind: whether it is to rescue Isabel one more time or whether she is thinking of Chloe, Phillip, Basenji, Mary Ann, all her friends, and those others not yet friends.

Behind her comes the pale young man, calling out that she must not risk herself or the baby . . . that she should let him do it, but Pooch doesn't hear, and, in fact, doesn't realize that she still has the baby on her back until she is halfway up the first flight of the back stairs. Then she feels its grip around her neck. Thinks, too late, to go back. Passing through that doorway again is out of the question by now. Besides, hasn't it been through everything with her: the dirt, the thirst, the hunger, the pound, cages, solitary confinement, even howling at the moon?

She twists her head to give it a lick on the cheek. "Whatever life brings, we'll share," she says, and "I can do no more than the best I can." Of course the baby can't understand all this except on an emotional level, but it calls her "Mama" for the first time. Then murmurs it over and over in her ear as she trots up the stairs.

★   ★   ★

Through all this confusion the three vice presidents are safely encased in their Early-Life pens and are being powdered, air-dried, rocked, and sung to. They have given up struggling with the machinery and now lie exhausted, letting themselves be tickled and petted. The explosions reach them only as dull *thunks*. They don't even wonder about them, having their own problems with this overzealous mothering.

All three men are beginning to feel that mothering itself may be a more powerful weapon than they had thought. It seems to them now more violent than bombs. They are overwhelmed by it. Each one decides that, when they are let out, they will launch a great campaign to be sure to keep motherhood in the hands of men who can deal with it. (They are sorry now that they gave first prize in mothering to the man who invented this pen.) They have come to believe that motherhood should be dealt out, even to infants, in small, insignificant doses so that it can always be held within reasonable bounds. It's sexy, too. They see that now, and they do not want to sink into that kind of softness, either. They will steel themselves against it and help other men to do the same. The inclination to sink into loving arms must be carefully modulated so that it doesn't get out of hand. How can there be any peace with such a force as this in the world? But if men can stick together, they will prevail against the softness. Meanwhile the vice presidents have no choice but to sink into the great pink breasts and be done to as the machine-mother wishes. It is hoped they will be let out *in time*.

CHAPTER XXI
Rescued

> The fourth [priest] carried the model of a left hand with the fingers stretched out, which is an emblem of justice because the left hand, with its natural slowness and lack of any craft or subtlety, seems more impartial than the right.
>
> *Robert Graves*

While the three vice presidents remain in their pens, the members of the Academy who had been restrained in harnesses, leashes, toddler straitjackets, or facsimiles have been freed by their comrades from across the street, with the help of the Rosemarys from the police department. Now they have made their way up the stairs so that at last all the creatures of every sort have made their way to the temporary safety of the roof. There is Pooch, the doctor, and Rosemary, Phillip, Cucumber, Valdoviccini, and even Isabel (who is growling and pacing and snapping out at mothers and Academy members alike—in her nervousness she seems to have reverted to her old "human" disposition). Fire engine sirens are heard in the distance, but they're not getting any closer. They are stuck somewhere out at the edge of the crowd. For the time being, however, all the creatures are safe.

It is a political moment, for here are the Academy of Motherhood members facing the mothers-to-be and quite outnumbered by them and their friends. The Academy members are wondering, now, if they shouldn't have been a bit less brusque in their treatment of the mothers—if they shouldn't have, for instance, warmed the specula, patted hands or paws now and then, been reassuring. Suddenly they understand the importance of small gestures and that indulging in them would certainly not have wasted significant amounts of time.

Beneath them, and above the street at the fourth-, fifth-, and sixth-story levels, the acrobats wait, relaxed, sitting sideways on their swings. They are dressed alike in brilliant blue with sequins of silver. The females among them (dressed similarly but with silver tiaras) are all halfway between human and chimpanzee, or gibbon, or orangutan. (The orange fur of these last contrasts beautifully with the blue of their costumes.) But ape or not, they all have such nice smiles, one feels sure that one can put one's life in their hands. Of course these acrobats were set up for an entirely different purpose: a daring rescue, yes — just as this will be — only now they will be rescuing everyone, friend and foe alike.

Up on the roof, in the flesh — or rather in the fur — stands the leader of the opposition, the largest and most abominable of all females. This is motherhood gone wrong! Rosemary has shed her policeman suit and stands there in all her terrible splendor. This is motherhood just as they've always suspected it was. Great and Terrible World-Mother. Big Mama. Venus of Willendorf no longer fitting in the palm of one's hand, but as she probably really was, maybe seven feet tall, and in this case with little beady eyes peering out from beneath furry brows.

Every time the wind changes, smoke is blown right onto the roof and some smoke is seeping up, here and there, through seams around the roof edges. So, amid coughing and wheezing, Rosemary asks both sides to make quick promises to love and honor, have and hold, in sickness and in health, till death do . . . and so forth, but just at the last minute, when everyone is supposed to say "I do," the Academy members say "I don't." They have realized that things must be done in a hurry, but why in a hurry the female's way? They know there's no time to bicker. So everything is left unresolved as they go about the business of rescuing each other.

The mounted heads, the bear and zebra rugs, and all the other disguises are piled up at the far edge of the roof to burn along with the building, a fitting funeral pyre for those poor, dear creatures whose skins and heads they are.

Then a strange thing happens . . . a kind of brilliance and a shaking, not just of the building because those on the ground feel it, too. Later the doctor will say that the explanation is quite simple, really, and has to do with star forces. It is merely a quake — a universe quake of some sort, a readjustment of galactic forces into a more stable equilibrium. And now, unless the earth should tip on its orbit or some such thing, all should be even better off than before.

Everyone feels that lurch except the swinging acrobats. Everyone sees it as a streak across the sky. It is a moment in which everything might change back to the way it always has been. In Pooch there are a few seconds of utter dogness, frightening her so that she feels her heart somersault. No, no, no! Humanity! She wants to join the humans.

She shuts her eyes, then opens them. All is as it just was. Only a few creatures out of place and those only by a yard or two. Perhaps one dwarf too many standing on the parapet. And there, the doctor is already kissing Phillip. Valdoviccini, holding hands with Chloe. One of the Academy members has his arms around Cucumber. A poem springs into Pooch's head.

"Bert," she says, for now she knows the pale young man's name is Bert. "Bert," she says again, because it's already her favorite name, and she asks him to listen to the poem. It's her first attempt at a more contemporary form:

Let the sunflower cast its vote
For rain. The cat for bird and tree.
The spider vote by weaving webs.
The bee by wax. Mouse by cheese.
The fox by being foxy.
Bats in clicks. The universe
By all things universal.
The moon by being in the sky.
The sky by blue. And I look
Into the eyes of someone I love,
And vote by five fingers on each hand!
Two legs! Ten toes!

"Well then, who *will* be the first to jump?"

Has John been standing on the wall all this time ready to help anyone who's willing to jump down into the arms of the acrobats? But they are all hanging back. Even with the net and the acrobats, it's a long, dangerous drop.

"Let's sing them down," Pooch says. "Let's pick a courageous aria. All can join in and even those on the ground can sing and play along with us." So they sing *Ritorna Vincitor,* and *Gloria all' Eggito,* and even *Why Do the Nations So Furiously Rage Together?* Then Bert does his *Toreador* song, still in his Papageno outfit. (Pooch falls in love with him all over again in that silly, romantic way she had promised herself never to do again. But why not, now that he seems to like her and to be so sweet? Besides it's too late. She is swept off her feet.)

Chloe jumps first because, as she says, she knows how to land. She turns three somersaults on the way down, showing off. The acrobats catch her and flip her over and down from one to another until they drop her safely into the net . . . on her feet, of course.

Valdoviccini insists on being second, but just before he jumps he gets Pooch's signature that she will become a member of the opera company and be coached by the best coaches in the city. She signs, this time, simply *Pooch.* From now on she will be her simple self and forget about trying to be Pucci. Though she feels a pang, she knows it is only for the loss of illusions.

Valdoviccini blinks at the name, then smiles and kisses her. She sees he understands. Then he jumps, a fat round ball, arms and legs out straight. Then comes Phillip. Again a graceful performance, utterly without fear. After her, the doctor. Just before he jumps he begins a quote from Marcus Aurelius, which, in order to save time, he finishes on the way down. It is rather muddled, but one can forgive him for not getting it quite right, considering the extenuating circumstances.

"Even if what befalls is unpalatable, receive it gladly, for it makes for the health of the universe. . . . What happens concerns yourself as a string in the tapestry of primordial causation. . . . To break off a particle from the continuous concatenation, is to injure the whole. . . ."

It is here that he jumps. He falls stiffly, as though standing at attention, rotating end for end.

". . . specific occurrences are ordered in the interests of our destiny," he says.

The acrobats pass him down in the businesslike way that he clearly prefers.

And now come down, in the arms of Cucumber, two of the newborn piglets, and after them, in the arms of an Academy member, the colt.

Now comes the mother of the four, holding the remaining piglet. Though she is quite large and pinkish and with thinning hair, one can see how she was mistakenly thought to be still completely human.

Then Mary Ann (one never did know whether tending toward duck or swan), squawking and flapping about so erratically it is clear that the acrobats will never be able to catch her. But then, just at the last moment, when a great "Ohhhhhh" of fear has already gone up from the crowd below, suddenly the flapping comes together in a graceful and powerful coordination. She *can* fly! Stretches out her long neck and beats her wings, and now there can be no doubt that she who stumbled over her own big feet, who tripped and staggered and waddled, is, after all, a swan, and air her element. She circles, honking her joy and her farewell, then heads north. She will not be seen again until next fall, and then only passing through.

So one by one they jump until they are all down except Pooch, Bert, John, Rosemary, and Isabel, who adamantly refuses to be lured into jumping even by the invigorating sounds of the music. Finally Pooch coaxes her to the edge with a gentle song instead. Yes, as wolverine she is more sensitive than ever she was before. Pooch is singing Micaela's song, *"Je dis que rien ne m'épouvante."* Perhaps Isabel remembers some high-school French from long ago, for she looks as if she understands every word.

But now there are big billows of smoke, some even coming up from the roof itself, right here where they stand. Rosemary is suddenly impatient and pushes Isabel over the side. Down she goes, twisting angrily and snapping at the air. She manages to bite the hands of two of the acrobats, and then tears holes in the net with her teeth before she can be chased out of it.

Bert has said that Pooch must go first, then he, then Rosemary, and then John. Pooch sees the logic in it. They kiss. Pooch's first real sexual, loving kiss. The baby, screaming with rage and trying to pull Bert away, grabs the Papageno topknot and bends it so that Bert looks a bit rakish. But below the tilted, drooping crest, Bert's tan eyes look out, concerned and kind as always. He turns to kiss the baby, but of course it pushes him away.

So Pooch stands upon the parapet, and, with refinement and grace, strikes a classical pose rather like an arabesque. She smiles, looking at Bert, and lets herself fall, the baby on her back crowing with delight.

The acrobats, though tired by now and some in pain from the bites on their arms, cannot resist whirling Pooch up again and again, and each time she takes an even more graceful pose than the time before.

But now more smoke than ever. Pooch can't even see the top of the building. Down comes another figure, a dim blob in the smoke. It's not a papageno but the clown, John. Where is Bert? As John drops into the net it tears in several places where Isabel had chewed it. This had not happened when Pooch fell into it because she, even with the baby, is so light. Pooch scrambles back up into the net with the idea of holding it together as well as she can or of breaking Bert's or even Rosemary's fall with her own body. But the circus clowns pull her away. "The baby!" they yell. "Don't forget the baby!" They know that will stop her, and of course it does.

Can it be, she wonders, that just when life is looking so happy she will lose the best thing about it?

But here he comes now. The acrobats are twirling him around, up and back. How can they do that at a serious moment like this, unless it is to keep him from death for another few seconds? Then one of them swings over to the little platform at the side and a moment later there is Bert, standing beside him, a bit off balance but safe, held tightly in the long arms of one of those gorgeous creatures, orange fur against the bright blue costume.

(Pooch feels a little twinge of jealousy.) The orangutan woman helps Bert to the rope and he slides down it, landing safely, only the worse for a couple of rope burns.

Of course Rosemary, up there with all this smoke, cannot see what has been happening below. Perhaps if she had waited, for the fire engines sound as though they're getting through at last. . . . But here she comes. She weighs far and away the most of any creature the acrobats have yet had to catch. Even the strongest of them cannot hold her. Down she goes, straight into the torn net and onto the street below almost as if there were nothing there at all to break her fall.

A great *Ohhhhhh* goes up from the crowd and then silence. Rosemary lies, a glistening, broken lump, but not dead. Dying, but not dead. She is trying to say something. Pooch leans near to her. There's blood on her white fur, especially around her face. Just as she begins to get a word or two out, the fire engines do get through. Their racket is tremendous and there's utter chaos as they push away all the creatures and the clowns and insist on taking over in their own way. Rosemary goes on speaking. Even though Pooch has extraordinarily good hearing still, she can make out very little. Yet they are words she will always remember: "Wisdom of the wild things," and, "You. You, yourself, and especially" — Rosemary says it, "Especially not win, or lose all." Pooch knows what Rosemary stands for, so it hardly matters that she can hear very little. "I will go on fighting," she tells Rosemary. She is thinking that, besides this good fight for the sake of all creatures, she will write poems about these things, and maybe even an opera. Yes, with Rosemary as the heroine, ending with a dance of fire as this fire right now, though it will have a better ending than all this confusion, firemen pushing everyone away and shouting at them and the sirens hurting her ears. She leans close to tell Rosemary about the opera, but Rosemary's eyes are blank. It's too late.

★　★　★

Now that the firemen are there, the fire is soon put out and the three vice presidents rise up from their pens like three phoenixes. But rescue has come, in a way, too late for them as well. One can see it in their eyes and the way they move. They are still hopelessly enmeshed in motherhood, as before, but now from the opposite point of view. If they continue as vice presidents, their influence on the Academy will be in an entirely different direction. However, Pooch feels that they will not be any less happy than they were before and maybe, with their newfound motherliness and sexuality, they will be even more so.

Pooch is hoping that (if the building survives) the Academy might become a haven for unwed creatures regardless of their backgrounds. Perhaps the members' room might be a room for both male and female regardless of funny noises or odd ways of lounging around. Pooch plans to have a memorial service for the mounted heads and the bear and zebra rugs with their friends and relatives attending, if such can be found. She herself will come to the ceremony to say good-bye even though she had not known any of the creatures personally.

But listen, now, to what those three vice presidents are announcing. They are saying that they will work hard on behalf of all females, and begin by bringing the measuring of time back to what it used to be — to a year of thirteen months and one day. They know that it was changed on purpose against women and adopted even though it is neither reasonable nor scientific. (They are ashamed that men instigated it.)

Also they want that one extra day of the year to be known as All Creatures Day and to be celebrated with music, balloons, kites, ice cream, firecrackers, popcorn, circuses, poems, free rides, art works, dancing, jokes, and all the other wonderful things. Hearing this, Pooch is thinking that, if everyone works hard to achieve it, every day of the year can be made more like this one great day will surely be.

Epilogue

*Et maintenant, parlez, mes belles, de
l'avenir, donnez-nous des nouvelles . . .
dites-nous qui nous aimera!*

Carmen

Of course Pooch and Bert marry and adopt the baby which, since its mother is in the aquarium and its father clearly unsuitable, is not hard to do. And of course they love it as though it were their own. Later they will have a litter of three: setters and all males, so there will be no hope that they might ever become human and artists in their own right, but Pooch will love them as much as anyone could love another creature, and she will give them every advantage to develop as fully as they possibly can. They will all three have wonderful, strong, vibrant voices, which she will delight in almost as much as she delights in her own. The baby will find them true brothers, and will never be jealous of them, but will delight in running with them in the woods and fields, baying now and then at the moon, and howling when Pooch vocalizes. Though the baby will never learn to sing, it will have a deep, abiding appreciation of music as well as of all arts, influenced by Pooch's example and teachings. It will grow up to write poems as good as or even better than Pooch's. Certainly more modern, strongly influenced by Kenneth Koch as well as Henri Michaux. (Of course it will grow out of biting other creatures except when absolutely warranted.)

Though it will take some time, the doctor will eventually persuade Phillip to marry him. They will have no offspring. Phillip will be sad about that even though she will have her career as a ballet dancer. Instead, she will love Pooch's puppies as

159

though they were her own. And the baby will call her Aunt Phillip.

Chloe and Valdoviccini will have a litter of their own and will give up altogether the apartment in the East Village. Strange to say, Pooch will be sad to see it and all the things in it go, though she knows it's for the best.

Pooch will continue with her psychotherapy, taking up where she left off several months ago with the daisies and such. She will never again allow herself to sleep on a doormat, unless of course it might benefit some other creature for her to do so. The psychologist will understand that a good bit of her personality is hereditary, her ancestors having been bred for generations for just such qualities as she possesses. She is, and will remain, basically, as stated in the official publication of the American Kennel Club: "The mild, sweet disposition characteristic of this breed, along with the beauty, intelligence, and aristocratic appearance it makes in the field and in the home, has endeared it both to sportsmen as well as all lovers of a beautiful, active, and rugged outdoor (companion)." But since she is human by now she'll be harder to live with, though there will be more rewards for doing so.

As she grows older Pooch will sing better than ever, and delight the world with her voice and her grace. Also she will continue, as she promised the dying Rosemary, to fight for the rights of all creatures, yet being careful to "not win." And she will write her opera, titled simply, *Rosemary: In Memoriam.* The two best arias in it will be "Oh, the Songs of Selves" and "Neither Conqueror nor Conquered; Neither Victory nor Defeat."

And what of the universe in general while "it is being woven out of light and at the speed of light"? One can, without a doubt, assume that its equilibrium is interconnected with all other manifestations, even as Marcus Aurelius said long ago. It is, in short, harmonious with itself. (Which is how Pooch is, as well as Bert, and how the baby grows up to be also.) And whatever it may be (which can be argued by the experts for a long time) or may come to be, it is recreating itself every fraction of a second, even as you and I. Of that we can be sure, despite appearances to the contrary.

"In the realm of light there is no time." That is said nowadays by the most modern of the physicists. If that is true, then that is how it is with Pooch and with Carmen and with all the others.